THE DEVIL'S

Gladys Maude Winifred Mitchell – or 'The Great Gladys' as Philip Larkin called her – was born in 1901, in Cowley in Oxfordshire. She graduated in history from University College London and in 1921 began her long career as a teacher. She studied the works of Sigmund Freud and attributed her interest in witchcraft to the influence of her friend, the detective novelist Helen Simpson.

Her first novel, *Speedy Death*, was published in 1929 and introduced readers to Beatrice Adela Lestrange Bradley, the heroine of a further sixty six crime novels. She wrote at least one novel a year throughout her career and was an early member of the Detection Club, alongside Agatha Christie, G.K Chesterton and Dorothy Sayers. In 1961 she retired from teaching and, from her home in Dorset, continued to write, receiving the Crime Writers' Association Silver Dagger in 1976. Gladys Mitchell died in 1983.

VINTAGE MURDER MYSTERIES

With the sign of a human skull upon its back and a melancholy shriek emitted when disturbed, the Death's Head Hawkmoth has for centuries been a bringer of doom and an omen of death - which is why we chose it as the emblem for our Vintage Murder Mysteries.

Some say that its appearance in King George III's bedchamber pushed him into madness. Others believe that should its wings extinguish a candle by night, those nearby will be cursed with blindness. Indeed its very name, *Acherontia atropos*, delves into the most sinister realms of Greek mythology: Acheron, the River of Pain in the underworld, and Atropos, the Fate charged with severing the thread of life.

The perfect companion, then, for our Vintage Murder Mysteries sleuths, for whom sinister occurrences are never far away and murder is always just around the corner …

GLADYS MITCHELL

The Devil's Elbow

VINTAGE BOOKS
London

Published by Vintage 2014

2 4 6 8 10 9 7 5 3 1

First published in Great Britain by
Michael Joseph Ltd in 1951

Vintage
Random House, 20 Vauxhall Bridge Road,
London SW1V 2SA

www.vintage-books.co.uk

Addresses for companies within The Random House Group Limited
can be found at: www.randomhouse.co.uk/offices.htm

The Random House Group Limited Reg. No. 954009

A CIP catalogue record for this book
is available from the British Library

ISBN 9780099583943

The Random House Group Limited supports The Forest Stewardship
Council® (FSC®), the leading international forest-certification organisation.
Our books carrying the FSC label are printed on FSC®-certified paper.
FSC is the only forest-certification scheme supported by the leading
environmental organisations, including Greenpeace. Our
paper procurement policy can be found at
www.randomhouse.co.uk/environment

MIX
Paper | Supporting
responsible forestry
FSC® C018179

Printed and bound in Great Britain by Clays Ltd, St Ives plc

INTRODUCTION

*

Of and Concerning a Corpse

'I'M NO SAYING I'm glad to see you, and I'm no saying I'm *no* glad to see you,' said Inspector Mactavish. 'Eh, weel, yon's the body.'

'And it was found on board a motor cruiser?'

'Aye. Moreover, it will be an English body. Ane o' these holiday-makers, no doubt. "See the whole o' bo'ny Scotland for fourrty guineas inclusive." ' His tone combined pity, censure and amused contempt in equal proportions.

'I suppose you know by this time who it was?' enquired Detective-Inspector Gavin of Scotland Yard, himself on holiday in Scotland.

'I'll refair you to Mrs. Lestrange Bradley here, wha has been briefed by the Home Office. She kens wha it was, and she kens why we brought the body back here.'

Mrs. Lestrange Bradley, a small, black-haired, yellow-skinned, elderly woman, waved a clawlike hand.

'Holiday-maker is right,' she agreed in a ·voice of surprising resonance and beauty. 'A passenger on a touring motor-coach. As it happens, I am lucky enough to possess copies of some documents connecting the young courier who accompanied the touring party with various incidents which may help us.' She turned her head and regarded the

7

dead body sombrely. 'A very nasty knock on the head,' she observed.

'Aye,' agreed Mactavish, 'yon's the weapon.'

'Almost anybody's weapon,' commented Mrs. Bradley, looking at a heavy stone without much interest. 'Well, I shall now add these documents to the pool of our common knowledge. They represent an uncensored source of information, except that, in the interest of the parties chiefly concerned, I have omitted the purple passages and have slightly emphasized the time-factor.'

'You've never tampered with evidence?' demanded Mactavish, scandalized.

'To the extent I have just now indicated, yes. I am under promise to Em, the owner of the documents in question'—she leered with horrid effect—'to keep some of the matter where it properly belongs—in the dark. Here you are. Make what you can out of these.'

She produced a bundle of typescript.

BOOK ONE

Excerpts from Dan to Em

*

'It is the common wonder of all men, how among so many millions of faces, there should be none alike: now contrary, I wonder as much how there should be any. He that shall consider how many thousand several words have been carelessly and without study composed out of twenty-four letters; withal, how many hundred lines there are to be drawn in the Fabrick of one Man, shall easily find that this variety is necessary.'

Sir Thomas Browne: *Religio Medici* (Part 2, Section 2)

---

[1]

I HAVE GOT the job, been briefed, and start to-morrow for bonny Scotland. There will be thirty-one passengers on the coach. There should be thirty-two, but two people turned in their reservations yesterday because one of them is ill. There was a waiting list for seats, but the agents have only been able to get rid of one place at such short notice because the others who wanted to go have fixed up elsewhere by this time.

The head courier informs me that I may be very glad of the empty seat, as it will enable me to change my place in the coach now and again. Supposing that I get stuck with some acidulated female with an unquenchable thirst for information, I shall find myself in complete agreement with him! Anyway, I look like being luckier than last year's

9

courier. When he came to load up it was discovered that the agents had sold his seat with the rest, and he did the whole fortnight's tour seated on an orange box just inside the doorway!

I don't know anything about any of the passengers yet except their names (which are on my list), and their home addresses (which are on a separate sheet marked *Confidential*).

There are several hundred rules and regulations about taking people on a coach tour, and I have had to learn them all! I always thought motor-coaches went where they liked, so long as they weren't obstructive, but this is far from the truth. We are licensed from county to county, must take only the roads we have permission to take, must not presume to deviate from the agreed route, must not do jaunts (we have to hire local transport if the passengers want to visit 'places of interest'), and we must enter and leave towns by the roads agreed to. I don't know what happens if these roads are up, or flooded, or if we lose our way. My driver has only done this trip once before, it seems, and you know how much *I* know of everything north of Yorkshire!

Well, I suppose I'd better pack. One small grip each is the total luggage allowance for the passengers, and as I have to take a boiled shirt and the soup and fish, I am allowed the same. I am told that if the passengers bring more than the allowance I must contrive somehow to get it stowed. The driver is supposed to do most of the heaving and hauling, but I have to give the directions. I also have to see that all the labels stay on!

We were late starting from Hal's Cross because it turned out that my driver had left his wallet and all his papers on the mantelpiece at his home, and he lives in Purley! So while he got busy on the telephone I had to see to all the luggage and get our clearance from the clerk at the coach station.

I soon discovered that it would be impossible to store all the suitcases in the coach's boot, enormous though this looked, so the only thing left to do was to stick the smaller cases under the seats. Nobody took to this idea.

One dear old girl named Miss Pew, very tall, thin and ladylike, and with whom I can see I'm going to have endless trouble, complained bitterly that she hadn't room for her feet, and a very stout, frightfully red-faced old fellow named Leese, who's got the seat next to mine and is going to take up quite his fair share of room, said loudly and belligerently that usually the passengers had to put up with the luggage down the centre gangway as well as under the seats, and that I 'wasn't to worry, cock,' about lugging it hither and thither. He then added in a terrific 'aside' to the people in the seat behind ours that his statement was a lie, but that he wasn't going to have a fine young fellow like me drag his something guts out for a something old cow like her! I foresee a certain amount of fun and games with these two, for, although the maiden lady claims to be deaf, she wears a doings in her lug and must have heard him.

Before we started, one of the high-ups from the firm came aboard and, having given my coach load the once-over, rather as though they were a schoolkids' outing who were not expected to behave themselves too well, he gave tongue as follows:

'Well, good people, good morning to you all!' (Confused greetings from the mob except from the old boy, who muttered, 'Communist stuff! Cut it out, will you?') 'You have a nice day to begin your trip. A beautiful day! Now I want you to know that everything has been done to ensure you a comfortable journey. First of all, I'm going to introduce Mr. Edwards, your driver. Albert Edwards in his baptism, but to us and to you—Bert. Bert's a good chap. A very good chap. He's a good driver, too.' (Nervous giggles from the coach and an answering *Ha! ha! ha!* from the high-up.) 'Yes, you'll be perfectly safe with Bert, won't they, Bert? Otherwise he would not be with us to-day. He would be where the good dogs go.'

The old chap: 'Battersea.'

The high-up: 'Ha! ha! ha! Very good! I can see you're a caution, sir! Take care, ladies! This gentleman is a *caution!* Well, now for your courier. This is your courier.' (Me!) 'He looks rather shy just now, but you'll soon cure him of that, ladies! He isn't our regular courier, who, as you all know, is our Mr. Spencer Caradoc. No, I'm afraid he isn't Mr. Caradoc, good people, but all the same, he is *very good indeed*, a real Stewart Macpherson. He knows all the answers. Ha! ha! ha! But this is his first trip with us, so I know you will all back him up. His name is Jeffries, but I know you won't hold *that* against him! Ha! ha! ha! George Jeffries. No, I did *not* say Judge Jeffries! Ha! ha! ha! ha! ha! Mr. *George* Jeffries. And Bert, your driver. Well, God-speed and good luck, you very, very fortunate people! How I *wish* I were going with you! But, there

Some of us must stay behind and do the donkey-work, or where would *you* be? Well, a pleasant holiday, good people. Good-bye, good-bye, *good*-bye!'

Having got that off the record, the high-up climbed down, Bert climbed up, I gave a last look round to make sure we had all the cargo aboard—the human kind, I mean—and off we drove. Bert seems a bit of an artist. He's good-tempered, too, on the road.

We had morning coffee at Steppenhall. Nice place with the largest Tudor fireplace I've ever seen. It seems that we are expected to be a complete democracy in microcosm on this coach. In other words, instead of oiling round to the back door for a pint, Bert and I have to sit with the customers. We picked our two left-hand front-seaters. Nice women, although I'd rather have had a drink.

One is good-looking, the other not. Both middle-aged, and both seem sensible. Know their way about, too. I think this trip is chickenfeed to both. Same address on the backs of their luggage labels, I noticed, so I suppose they're a couple of what Maurice Richardson calls 'jovial collar-and-tie spinsters.' One is named Baird and the other Carter. Right amount of luggage, ancient but good. Easy to get on with, too, which is more than I am going to be able to say in favour of some of this menagerie. That much I know already, apart from the Leese and the Pew.

After we left Steppenhall there was some dullish driving up the Great North Road before we arrived in Stanbridge for lunch. Wonderful old coaching inn with lots of stabling (now used as garages, of course), and the house itself joined on to a bit of a thirteenth-century monastery. The main building mostly seventeenth and eighteenth century.

Vast place. A two-hundred-year-old wistaria in the garden, a marvellous old gate-house with porter's spy-
window, and a couple of ancient pumps in the yard.

We were given a private dining-room and a very fat
waitress. I don't think she liked us much, and, as she
seemed to be single-handed on the job, I don't know that
I blame her. Anyway, the lunch was all right, although
Miss Pew complained that she was given apple rice when
she had asked for ice-cream. She's the sort who'll be served
out with the wrong pair of wings when she gets to glory
(or the wrong toasting fork if it's t'other place), and then
there'll be a row about that! I wish Leese would give up
trying to keep her in order, though. There'll be murder
done if he continues to refer to her as Mrs. Rabbit-Guts,
because I *know* she can hear him.

I sat at lunch with the old chap and two *very* bright
young things (aged about thirty-five) named Nordle and
Pratt. Both bloody-awful but Pratt worse than Nordle.
However, I did the gallant. Bert remarked (unnecessarily)
when he met me walking them round the garden afterwards, that I'd better look out or one of them would have
me nobbled before we got to Gretna. Screams of delight
from both the medium and the small female. (Pratt quite
the runt of her family, I should think. She's quite repul-
sively *petite*. Maybe it accounts for her behaviour.) Your
sex, on the whole, shocks me deeply! *Darling* Em!

Had enough time, after settling our bill and the communal tip, (the passengers pay an all-in sum and only tip
on their drinks, and not all of them always then), to get a
glimpse of the town. Thirteenth-tenderly-changed-to-
fifteenth-century church with a really lovely roof. Must

have been a monastic church when built. It's enormous, and outside, to the south, there are tantalizing remains of the cloisters and, further away, a chunk of the monastery guest-house. The town climbs a steep hill, and on the left, after you've crossed the bridge, there's a beautiful Norman doorway, now leading nowhere. The townspeople call it Heaven's Gate. Rather apt, or am I a cynic?

Back to the coach to find Bert swearing because somebody, in turning, had marked his paint. Still, a change from Miss Pew's complaints, if only because expressed in more definite dactyls. Off we went northwards to Arrowbridge. Had tea at an old inn near Barnsley. I had just time to slide to the table of Miss Baird and Miss Carter before the Pratt could think quickly enough to pat a vacant chair. Bert winked at me and sat down in it! God bless Bert. He's a happily-married man with two kids, a dog, a cat, a parrot, and a fountain pen for filling in his Pools. He calls his wife the Old Woman and our bus Sweetheart. What a man!

[3]

My first job, as soon as we arrived at our first real stopping-place, was to greet the manager and lead the customers to the hotel office to get their keys. Our two front-seat clients, Miss Baird and Miss Carter, got the best bedroom. By the way, I discovered, during the afternoon, that they are authors. I haven't the foggiest idea what sort of thing they write—it could be anything from detective stories to modern poetry. I feel, somehow, that they are not blue-stockings, but even that is open to doubt now that every second bloke who holds a Chair at a university seems to talk Old Kent Road.

Miss Pew, who also has a double room which she shares with her unfortunate companion Mrs. Adderley, decided to lodge a complaint—about the seventy-fifth up to date! Why, she wanted to know, buttonholing me directly after dinner, should two younger and healthier women—the Baird and the Carter—be given a bedroom on the second floor while, although she also was sharing, she had to go up to the third? I promised to do what I could, but pointed out that the party was only there for one night, and that the hotel had a lift to all floors. She demanded to be told whose duty it would be to rescue her in case of fire. Well, there *are* genuine pyrophobes, I know—and a blasted nuisance they are to their friends and relations—but I decided that Miss Pew was not among their number. However, I replied that in case of fire the courier was in honour bound not to lose any of the passengers.

She accepted this heroic declaration with a snort. For your private information, Em, dear, I shall probably murder her before the trip is over. It is rather a temptation to toy with the thought at this hotel, as outside the bathroom I mentioned there is a 'light' to the dining-room. This light is covered with wire netting, and unless you open the bathroom window at the bottom (which I did because I wanted to pitch out a drowned cigarette end), I don't believe anyone would ever find the body until it began to decompose, and by the time the murder was discovered we should be some hundreds of miles away, and there probably wouldn't be a clue.

The expected has happened. I've had my first spot of bother. Nothing terrible, though, thank goodness. It was this way. First thing this morning the management complained that four of my tribe dined at the wrong table last night. I said yes, I knew. What about it? As a matter of fact, the culprits were Miss Baird and Miss Carter, and Commander and Mrs. Parks, who made a foursome in a part of the room which had not been allotted to our coach-load. Parks is a retired naval bloke and his wife is a very charming Scotswoman.

These four, not being accustomed to communal holidays, had walked into the dining-room when they were ready, and asked for a table. The head waiter didn't realize they belonged to the clan, so he placed them nicely in a window.

The management this morning turned terse, and pointed out that they received us 'as a distinct favour,' and that we must keep to the book of words, and go where we are told. I didn't like their manner and turned awkward. I told them that the only reason they could keep their heads above water at the present time was because they had the chance of the coach parties. I added that I should refer their attitude to my office. They retorted (in polite language), 'And your Aunt Fanny, too,' at which my natural urge to be offensive got the better of me, and I replied spiritedly with a chunk of sheer Brazenose.

After that we became quite matey, but, unfortunately, the whole thing had been overheard by the inexpressible Pratt girl, and also by the old fellow Leese. *She* approached me, giggling, and said I was a naughty man! *He* (the old pest) retailed the whole dialogue to the coach at large as soon as we set off this morning. Miss Pew sniffed and talked loudly of fortune's favourites, meaning the Baird and the Carter, and added, for good measure, that she supposed that if *she* drank like a fish (the party of four had one bottle of Chateau Neuf du Pape at dinner, followed by brandies with their coffee) she might get preferential treatment too. Fortunately this struck the Baird and the Carter as being mildly comical, an attitude which relieved *me* but which the old duck didn't deserve. Sometimes I wish there were some polite version of kicking ladies in the pants!

[5]

I shall turn in now. I'm right at the top of the house in a tiny attic about level with the tops of the hills. We have Priesthope Hill and Windlestraw Law to the back of us, and Glenlath Hill and Dun Rig in front of us. It's a lovely spot, and heavenly, wonderfully quiet. My six hundred (they seem quite as many as that when I've got to get them all bedded down and shepherded into meals!) are asleep, I trust, by now, and I feel as though I'd better follow suit. I'm glad the holiday secretarying goes well. I'd rather like to meet your employer. I was at school with a fellow called Bradley, but I don't suppose there's any connection. He played the fiddle rather decently, but was otherwise quite normal. He had a cousin who used to keep pigs near a place called Stanton St. John, in Oxfordshire. I went there once. Rather good.

P.S. (*Next morning.*) Find that I've given you no idea of yesterday afternoon. Seems a pity to leave anything out, in spite of what old Montacute, our history beak at school, used to say! So I'm up early to write this. We crossed the Border soon after two o'clock yesterday afternoon after driving across the wildest country I think I've ever seen except in Spain. Heather everywhere, no fences, suicidal sheep, and all the time the thrill of knowing that at an invisible barrier, as intangible and as real as the Equator, we should pass from England into Scotland. Childish! I don't suppose any of my flock turned a hair. They accept everything as included in the bill!

We all got out of the coach at Carter Bar. There are several snapshotters aboard, and this was their first real chance. The view was so wide that I don't know what they've managed to get. Old Leese has a camera he won in a raffle twenty-five years ago. The unspeakable Miss Pratt possesses a fairly respectable ciné-camera—a gadget which has its dangers, believe me, on a communal trip like this! The naval chap, Parks, has a super Zeiss—a lovely thing. I wouldn't mind it myself. Neither of our literary ladies takes photographs. Miss Carter informs me that she can buy the views she wants on picture postcards. She and Miss Baird are the most intelligent people on board (except for Bert and me!), and the most kindly and unselfish are a very nice couple named Wells. They have brought their niece along, a very bright, clever kid of eighteen who pulls my leg and treats me, in general, as an uncle. If only Miss Pratt would consider treating me as a nephew! Oh, *Lor!* That girl!

All the same some of my flock very nearly make up for

some others. Even Miss Pew is beginning to settle down a bit. She's given Mrs. Hocking a recipe for making damson cheese! When she gets to the stage of asking old Leese (by the way, I've contrived to get a reasonably fair share of the front seat by putting a tin of tobacco in my right-hand trouser pocket) to explain the game of darts to her, I shall consider my little holiday well spent.

[6]

We are at Scotstone all to-day and to-morrow. I've been getting more of the gen from Bert about these tours. We make them to fit the hotels, and not the hotels to fit in with where we want to go. We would have had to spend to-morrow here, anyway, because of the Scottish Sabbath, but, as it happens, that really suits us. It will make a change from travelling all the time, and the country round about looks pretty good. The Pratt tried to sound me about taking her for a morning walk to-day, but fortunately I was promised forth for an early swim with young Cathleen (the niece) and Miss Carter, so I was able to fob the Pratt off in a genteel manner which, I trust, did not hurt her feelings.

This place is some sort of hydro., and although it's almost given up 'the waters' in favour of dinner-dances for the local residents, the swimming bath is still a feature, and they warm the water even in summer. The hotel itself is a great, important-looking chunk of masonry half-way up a hill. I forgot to tell you that I went out for a stroll after dinner last night and made friends with a goose-girl.

She was about fifty-six years old, had a gaggle of goslings and some geese at the bottom of a well-kept garden, was very lame, very dignified, very friendly and very intelligent. If ever I leave you for another, it will probably be for her, so don't say I didn't warn you.

By the way, two or three of the customers are suffering quite badly from travel sickness. I find I'm quite sympathetic, and even feel rather worried about them, especially a fellow named Wrenn, who's just had a rather serious operation. His wife's very worried indeed, and says she hopes he'll get over the sickness and be able to finish the tour. I hope so, too. I don't a bit want to leave anyone behind, especially as I'm not at all sure that this place could accommodate them. The manager says they're full up with coach parties until the end of September.

There was a real artist at work on the river here yesterday evening, and I've been lent the manager's trout rod, so I'm going out now to prospect! This bloke I saw was using an Iron Blue Dun, which I should have thought cranky at this time in the season, but was doing wonders with it. All the same, I'm going to try a Medium Olive, but with what success I know not, as so far I've only fished in Welsh brooks where the trout go six to the pound, and in England would be thrown back with a shudder.

Reading the book of rules for the umpteenth time, I discovered this morning that I have to make an announcement as to the necessity, if it seems to arise, of donning the soup and fish. The entry, believe it or not, reads as follows:

'When at the definitely holiday-type grandiose three-star hotels (*cf.* particularly those at Scotstone and Blaneden) where after-dinner ballroom dancing is the norm, the

courier should take the opportunity at tea-time of attach-
ing himself to the largest party, preferably a mixed
gathering, and should remark with apparent casualness
that he proposes to wear full evening costume for dinner.
It will be found that this hint will be conveyed by the eager
gleaners to the rest of the coach company without delay.
On no account, however, should notice of any kind be
taken if passengers attend dinner or evening function in
undress. It should be borne in mind that many ladies when
travelling consider a light summer garment sufficient
change of attire for evening wear. The courier himself,
however, must never follow the lax custom of merely
exchanging a bow tie for his cravat, but should appear, *as
he has promised*, in full gentleman's evening wear, so that he
can take his place with assurance at table or on the dance
floor. The courier at all times must set the tone of the
party.'

It says nothing about having a bath, but I've had one,
just the same!

This morning I caught and landed three nice brown
trout, but had no luck with the Medium Olive, so exchanged it for a Blue Watery Dun. There's no doubt the
fishing here is marvellous. Gave the trout to the cook at
the hotel. I dined with the two Parks, so we each had one.
The management had the tact to slip everybody else a bit
of grilled haddock to match, so the Pew, for once, voiced
no complaint except to tell me that trout are poisonous!

We all went on an outing this afternoon. It was a great
success. We got our coach-load quite easily. Old Miss Pew

decided not to come (having previously bullied the Adderley into being one of the deputation!), and the unspeakable Pratt and Co. went to Edinburgh to do some shopping; so we had a nice comfortable trip with old Leese leaning heavily against me, fast alseep, most of the time!

When we went down to dinner this evening I could see the point of the soup-and-fish. All the staying guests (as distinct from us birds of passage) were togged up in full war-paint. There were dress kilts, buckled shoes, velvet jackets, clan brooches, magnificent sporrans, the most smashing stockings, dirks and *sgian dubhs* (or isn't that the Gaelic plural?). Our lot were thrilled, particularly the ladies, but, after dinner, when we all went along to the ballroom, most of us gave one aghast and terrified glance at an eightsome reel which was going on, and crawled abjectly away to the lounge. The Scots must get a frightful kick out of giving the English an inferiority complex. Besides, they're the only nation except the Red Indians where the males get it all their own way in matters of dress. No wonder they've conquered the earth.

Niece Wells and I braved it out, and had a waltz and a couple of foxtrots, for, luckily, these decadent gyrations alternated with the more spirited heel-toe-and-yelping of reels and strathspeys. Naturally enough, Parks and his Scottish wife were well in the swim. There's no doubt the Caledonians are a tough lot when it comes to dancing, and, in any case, there's nothing so Highland as the Lowlands! It will all be over by midnight, though. We do not encroach upon the Sabbath.

The vicious Pratt and her satellite Nordle apparently had a *screamingly* funny time in Edinburgh ciné-photographing the natives. 'But a *screamingly* funny time, my dear!' Pratt shrieked this out all through dinner. I wish an All-Caledonian tram could have run over both of them, especially the winsome wee Pratt. Even the Nordle is getting slightly peeved with her, and if some of the more elderly dames see very much more of her they'll burst!

What makes things worse is that it has begun to rain and to blow. In fact, I thought the hotel windows were going to be blown in. Miss Pew sniffed a bit, and said that she supposed it always rained in Scotland, and that we must now expect this kind of weather for the next ten days, and that she hoped Bert's windscreen wiper was working, because she had already purchased her grave in England and it would be ridiculous to die in a foreign country!

Some of the men, I fancy, were not sorry for an excuse to sit about the hotel reading the Sunday papers—incidentally, I gather that Sunday papers here are still regarded as an innovation directly sponsored by the devil —while their wives and the other ladies were busy exchanging knitting patterns, snob-talk and life-stories.

It is extraordinary how much we already seem to know about one another. We know that Mr. Viccars, of the back seat, is a schoolmaster and teaches history. This, of course, terrifies me, and I've spent quite a bit of to-day looking up facts I thought I knew. I used to imagine that the only tourists with a thirst for information were Americans, but this party yearns for it, too, and a woman named Durdle embarrasses me very much by thanking me loudly and shrilly for every sentence I let fall. She manages to make it sound like *Liar*—or could that be my nervous imaginings?

Anyway, to continue: we know that Viccars' wife teaches needlework at an evening institute. (Miss Pew has already commissioned a set of underclothes which she thinks she will get on the cheap. My summing-up of Mrs. Viccars causes me to think this very unlikely.) We also know that one of the Misses Tooley is in the Civil Service, and that the other designs clothes for the ballet. (Not bad girls, these two. Very sporting and jolly in a nice sort of way, and great favourites with everybody.)

We also know that the fat Mrs. Hocking lost her husband in a car crash and was left rather well off, and that her sister, Mrs. Amesby, fairer in colouring and very nearly as fat, keeps a baker's and confectioner's shop which her husband can manage with the help of their niece while Mrs. Amesby is on holiday.

So far we know nothing of Miss Bernard and her friend Miss Moxon, except that they 'did' the Derby winner this year—although whether they 'did' it in the accepted or in the Leon Cortez sense we haven't gathered. I don't like the Bernard much. She's empty and silly and sometimes naively coarse. She's got too much hair, a messy mass of musmonic mildew which gives her the appearance of having slept under a rather damp haystack, and of having come away with most of the hay on her head. Besides, underneath the silly emptiness I feel there is something rather 'orrid, although I don't in the least know what. The other one, the Moxon, seems all right, although not my type.

The rain is getting on my nerves. Besides, I'm sure the management here ain't any too keen on having us use up all the chairs and settees in the lounge. Further to that, some of the flock are apt to ask for rather unpopular drinks such as tea and cocoa at *definitely* unpopular hours! We're rather a teetotal lot, as it happens, and although that may be all to the good in one sense, it doesn't help in other ways, as perhaps you can imagine.

Oh, well! The hills are nothing but a deep green mist, the foreground is a depressing grey, the tennis courts are flooded and the swimming pool has been closed since nine this morning. The Baird and the Carter wined me last night—a respectable vintage, too!—so I shall now proceed to cocktail them before dinner—not that I can afford it, but *noblesse oblige*.

By the way, we have a chain-smoker on board. I don't know where her supplies come from. She must have brought her suitcase full of them! She's an unfocussed-looking, darkish woman named Mrs. Cassock. The Wells, bless them, are nice to her, but nobody else likes her a bit. Her seat-mate, a sentimental-seeming but, I suspect, tough specimen, aged forty-ish, I think, has already asked me to get somebody to change seats with her. A few discreet and tactful inquiries round and about among the party have elicited the fact that there isn't a hope. I broke this to her in my best manner, but she simply shrugged shoulders nearly as wide as my own, and looked down her nose, giving an impression of being a curious cross between Chaucer's Prioress and a Rugby football forward. *Definitely* anti-social.

I foresee trouble in the future, but it's no good meeting

it half-way. I've told this woman—Cann by name—that she can have the middle place on the back seat if she likes. However, she doesn't like. Says she couldn't stand the smell of Mrs. Parks' perfume. Says all scents make her feel sick. As she herself smells decidedly doggy, perhaps this is true. Anyway, Mrs. Parks wouldn't like *her* much, either.

[8]

It's fine to know that you are going on so well, and that you still like your old lady. Rather queer that she *should* be related to Denis Bradley, because it's really a very ordinary name.

Anyway, I'm glad Mrs. Lestrange Bradley neither beats nor starves you. I won't, either, when you live with me. Tell her not to have any murders to look into while you're with her. You and the corpses in the library don't mix and mingle at all.

Oh, Lord! It's still raining, and we leave at nine sharp for Edinburgh, where we tour the city until lunch-time. I then cart such as will to see St. Giles', and leave the rest of the mob (most of them, I hope) to their own devices until tea, and to-night we sleep at Blaneden.

[9]

It rained all the way to Edinburgh, but everybody seemed quite cheerful except our chain-smoking Mrs. Cassock. *She* was extremely morose. Said she didn't want to go to Edinburgh, didn't like her place in the coach, and had seen a rat run across her bedroom floor. She spent the first hour of the journey muttering darkly of these and more obscure matters. Miss Cann, who shares her seat, is getting more and more nervous and unhappy.

We reached Edinburgh at a quarter to eleven, cut out the usual coffee and biscuits and drove straight to Holyrood Palace. Mary Queen of Scots' apartments looked too small and cramped to be true, but I must say I liked the wood carvings in some of the other rooms.

We saw the Castle, too, and, of course, the War Memorial, and the view of the Firth of Forth was grand.

Bert did a cigarette crawl while we were 'doing' the Castle, and got a hundred and forty. He also repaired the broken handle of a handbag and got a recalcitrant lighter to work. He's much more popular than I am, although his private name for our coach-load is the Zoo Picnic, and for Miss Pew, (when he's tired), that Snotty Old Penguin. I *could* tell you his private title for the Pratt girl, but perhaps you're not quite old enough to hear it.

[10]

We've arrived in Blaneden, not very far from Dunblane. This is a grand place in every way. Good hotel, good grub, glorious walks. I got up at a quarter to seven this morning and went for a constitutional. The country here is much more open than around Scotstone, although it is still pretty hilly. I didn't get very far, because it was all too good and too interesting. I left the hotel and struck up the hill towards some woods.

It was the most marvellous morning. When I got to the woods I stopped for a minute and just stood quite still while a red squirrel sat up about two yards away from me. Then a blackbird sang and apparently warned him, for, in a couple of terrific bounds, his tail floating, he reached a tall tree and was half-way up the trunk. He paused a second, then scampered up into the branches and came out on the end of a bough to have another look at me.

There was a broad grassy ditch under some beeches beside a fence which cut the wood off from a meadow, and I saw dozens of rabbits, mainly young ones, playing about there. I watched them for three or four minutes, and then I trod on a stick. No more rabbits.

I crossed over the road after that and walked among the pine trees until I came up against a stone wall. I didn't like to climb it because there was an extremely new-looking motor-caravan just on the other side from where I stood, so I headed off to the left and soon got back on to the road.

The slope was steep and I was walking between two meadows. In one of them a Buff Orpington hen was foster-mothering six goslings. It was really funny to see her get between them and me, clucking at them nervously and fussily chivvying them away.

The lane ended at a farm. I snooped around for a bit, as there seemed to be nobody about, but a bloomin' great hound began to bark, so I judged it wiser to push off. I didn't want to be found trespassing. It was all too good for that.

On the way back I took to the woods again, and, believe

it or not, I came upon a great sandy fellow of a hare. What he was doing among pine woods heaven only knows. Nor did he seem in any particular hurry to depart. He sat up and looked at me, and I looked back at him. Then he shook his head in a human sort of way, as though he hadn't met my species before and didn't think much of it now that he had, and loped off in a dignified manner towards a glade which I could see through the trees.

I followed slowly—I wouldn't have scared him for the world; he might have been a witch, for all I knew—and the pine trees thinned and there was a great welter of bright pink willow-herb, and beyond it a gate into deciduous woods with a cart-track running through them.

Such evidence of civilization didn't fit, so I turned in my tracks and got back among the pine-trees. It was heavenly for about ten minutes; at the end of that time I was entirely lost. All the trees looked exactly alike and I couldn't remember where the road was.

I decided that the hare *must* have bewitched me, because I was positively certain that the wood was only a small one. However, I could hear the sound of the little brook—beg pardon, burn—which had been bubbling beside me as I walked from the hotel up the hill, and so I stood still until I was sure I had located the sound. Then I made for it.

Of course I came out beside the same stone wall and the same motor-caravan as before, only this time there was a spivvy-looking, although somewhat unshaven, bloke standing beside it talking to two of our party, Parks and Peel. Mrs. Peel, I suppose, was still in bed.

If I haven't mentioned these Peels before it's because I

didn't realize at first that they were husband and wife. One sits beside the ghastly Pratt female and the other on the seat in front, next to the almost as ghastly Miss Nordle. Near the beginning of our tour I made just one (abortive) attempt, at Peel's instigation, to get either Pratt or Nordle to change seats, so that the husband and wife could sit together. That was the first time I realized that they *were* husband and wife. Both the Pratt and the Nordle turned the idea down flat, and, although I loathe their shrieks of laughter, their silly faces, *all* their clothes, their disgustingly-bad, plastery make-up, their ugly knobbly knuckles and their nasty wet palms, (one has the one and the other the other), still, as a just and fair-minded man, I'm not above admitting that I don't blame them for standing firm. After all, they booked their two left-hand inside seats last February, and the Peels were mere haphazard Mayflies, so the booking stands and the two pairs don't speak. Nice for me, but I don't give a hoot!

Peel was a bit shirty about it when I broke the news that he and the missus must stay put, so much so that I had to restrain myself from giving him a punch on the nose. He told me he usually spent the season yachting at Cowes with his old friend Sir Teetery-Taw, (sorry, but I didn't get the name), but that Girlie (the rather odd *soubriquet* he sees fit to bestow upon his repulsive and over-dressed squaw) thought she'd like 'a bit of a change,' but there hadn't been time to book up anything interesting, and now he was sorry he'd come, especially with a courier who couldn't fix things. He added that he'd missed a very good Cricket Week, too, with his noble friend.

Rude words leapt to my tongue, but I held many of

them back. I merely told him he'd only himself to thank
if his holiday wasn't to his liking. I don't think he loves
me very much, and I wish Parks didn't like *him*, so when I
saw them in conversation I made a noise like a grass-snake
and slid gently away among the trees. Next thing I knew,
I was on top of a high, steep, red-earth bank, and there
below me was my lane, and striding along it at a most
surprising rate was our Miss Durdle. She's the one who
always thanks me for any information I pass on to the
clients. I don't like her much—she reminds me, for some
strange reason, of Mrs. Dyer, 'the infamous baby-farmer
of Reading.' Anyway, she confided to me one tea-time
(I'm supposed to change my table for every meal) that she
has been saving up for five years to do this trip because she
felt it was educational!

She spends hours reading my guide book to make sure
she's getting every ounce of value for her money. She
checks the route with me, keeps a list of all the things she
has to eat and drink, and nearly drives Bert dotty with
questions about his petrol consumption so that she can
work out how many miles we go to the gallon. Needless to
say, she keeps an enormous diary and writes it up in the
lounge every evening after dinner.

She doesn't usually venture beyond the hotel gardens
when we get a chance of a walk, because she hears of 'such
dreadful things happening to quite *elderly* people nowadays, and, after all, she herself is only forty,' so I was rather
surprised to meet her walking between the wild woods on
her lonesome and at such a pace, and at such an early hour.
I will say, however, that she did seem glad to see me. We
toddled matily back to breakfast and discussed the

Scottish countryside and Jessie, the Flower of Dunblane.

I spent the rest of the morning inspecting the town and the cathedral in company with Mr. Togg, Miss Macklin, old Mrs. Binns and Robert, aged fifteen. Robert is decidedly an odd youth—or else I'm already out of touch with the rising generation! He addresses his relative punctiliously as Grandmamma, shows her every possible courtesy, gets up when women blow over to where he is sitting, opens doors for them, and calls every male on board Sir, including Bert, who gets horribly embarrassed and calls him Sir in return. His chief hobby, he informs us (he has several), is going up steps. In a moment of confidence this morning, whilst we were standing on the terrace waiting for the ladies to join us, he was good enough to enlarge upon this whim. It seems that he has perfected a technique of opening locked doors to church towers so that he can ascend to the heights. Why he hasn't broken his neck years ago I can't think, many church towers being kept locked, I believe, because they are definitely unsafe.

He has a long list also of churches which still possess a rood staircase, and a black list of those in which this has been bricked up! He has little interest in crypts, he tells me. It is only *up* that he wants to go. Coming down is a mere necessity and not interesting. He's certainly a change from the stamp-collecting, engine-numbering, aeroplane-spotting brigade. I rather like him.

He acted as guide when we got to the cathedral, and incorporated in his information a short history of the reign of King David I, by whom this cathedral was founded. In his grandmother's presence he merely bestowed on the

B

door of the tower a meditative, speculative glance, but I have a theory that this afternoon, while I'm conducting a party to the Trossachs, he will be up on the parapet, adding another scalp to his collection. I anticipate that as he hasn't broken his neck so far, he'll probably break it on this tour! I think I'll recommend Doune Castle to him. My guide book says it has two towers, both of which command extensive views, so presumably they're safe to ascend. Anyway, as there seems to be some idea that one gives a gratuity for the privilege of viewing Doune Castle, somebody must be in charge there, and I would defy even Robert to get past a Scottish caretaker and into any part of the building which isn't supposed to be open to the public.

[II]

Our peculiar Mrs. Cassock hasn't smoked for two days now. I thought she'd got through her supplies and so offered her my case while we were waiting to go in to dinner. She took out a cigarette, looked at me with the most horribly crafty expression on her somewhat extraordinary face—she's all puffy and bloated and sallow—and pulled the fag slowly to pieces. I was rather astonished, but passed it off with the light laugh, not knowing what else to do. Parks came to my rescue, made her a bow, put a small black cheroot between her teeth, lit it for her, told her in his best naval-officer-on-duty voice to smoke it slowly, and lugged me into the bar, away from her.

There, over a gin and tonic, he put it up to me. Hadn't I noticed that there was something definitely odd about the woman? His wife was getting worried about it. I mumbled something about chain-smoking and nerves, and then he let me have it.

'She's crazy,' he said. 'And by crazy I mean crazy, and I'm not talking U.S., but plain, straightforward English. That woman is literally mad. My missus spotted it much sooner than I did, and she's a Scotswoman, as you know, and not fanciful. You'll have to do something about it. I wouldn't be surprised if she's dangerous.'

I asked him what the hell I *could* do. He didn't know, so we decided to wait upon events—not that that was much comfort! Well, this hotel goes in rather impressively for flowers, and on the mantelpiece near the Cassock's table there was a whacking great vase of mixed blossoms, and what does the Cassock do but march straight over to this eye-taking vase and very deliberately smash it! Just that. Right down in the hearth. No question of accident; just picked it up and slammed it down, crash! And then, like some blinking Brer Rabbit, she laughed and laughed and laughed.

Of course, we shall all be slung out, and, if we are, I haven't the first idea of what to do. There's only one other hotel in the place, and that couldn't accommodate us all, even if it had no other visitors. Besides, my push would legitimately complain.

Mrs. Parks and that darling Mrs. Wells got the Cassock upstairs and into bed, pushed her outside a large bromide, and came downstairs with their fingers crossed. The management have just rung my room. I'll have to go down and face the music. Pray for my soul!

Well! Wonders never do cease, no matter what the pessimists say! I've been interviewing the entertainments manager, a rosy, rotund sort of chap, MacFie by name, the image of a youthful Mr. Pickwick. *It doesn't matter about the vase.* The hotel is fully covered by insurance. His wife, who does the flowers, has always hated that particular piece of crockery and is glad to see the last of it. *I am not to worry!* Eccentric visitors not objected to . . . it gives the residents something to talk about and gingers up the staff. . . . All with a kindly pat on the back, I might tell you. Can you beat it? I wish I knew what to do about the Cassock, all the same!

Blow Parks! This having been a free day (and I shan't be at all sorry when we set out on our travels again—it's easier!) the mob deployed in various directions in search of entertainment. Nearly everybody went on the excursion I fixed up to Loch Katrine and the Trossachs. I suppose it sounded fairly attractive, as a boat trip on the loch and tea on its shores were included. Nothing would suit Parks, however, but to toddle off to the sea. Not the proper sea, either, mark you, where he could have paddled his tootsies, eaten ice-cream, seen a Punch and Judy show, bought some cockles, put a penny in the slot to see what the butler saw, and otherwise renewed his childhood memories. No. Nothing like that. Not even a little boat

and a local boatman for a spot of fishing. Not even a fun
fair or a pin-table or a shooting gallery. Not even a
shrimping net and his trousers turned up to the knee while
he splashed earnestly about in low-tide pools and little
crabs bit his big toe.

What that black-hearted ex-Commander has done is to
sneak off to Leith and hire a large motor-boat in which he
proposes to catch the tide to-morrow evening, cruise
round the coast, and meet us at Aberdeen the second
night we are there. Informs me he's done it before and
can find berths for at least half a dozen of the other
passengers provided they're willing to work their way—*i.e.*
help pay for the hire of the boat and take turns at cooking
the grub. He says the boat belongs to a friend of his, and
he's got her cheap. He says the weather's just right if it
stays like this, and the wind is nice and steady. I hope it
blows him overboard! Dash it, I'm *responsible* for the brute,
let alone for the idiots he's proposing to mulct of their
passage-money. I've a jolly good mind to wish Cassock,
Pratt, Pew and old Leese on him. That 'ud learn him!
Curse his sea-boots and blister the ends of his toes! I *know*
there's going to be trouble. I can feel it blowing this way.

[14]

We've had a far from dull day, one way and another.
I went out for before-breakfast exercise and covered five
miles of hilly walking in an hour and ten minutes. (Downhill coming back. Honesty compels this admission.) This
morning we had a bit more excitement from our auld

acquaintance Mrs. Cassock, who did *not* accompany the seafarers. They went off to-night after dinner.

Please thank Mrs. Bradley, by the way, for her information *re* apparent melancholiacs. When they begin smashing things they're probably getting dangerous, are they? What a comforting thought! But there's one thing, it won't be me she'll go for. She doesn't like me. She told me so this morning, and loonies always attack their loved ones first, or so I've heard. But I'd better begin at the beginning.

She got off to a bad start. Tossed her cup on to the floor and laughed loudly as it crashed, got up from the table before anybody else had so much as tasted their haddock, and retreated at a sort of gallop.

I followed her out of the dining-room, but she merely legged it upstairs and disappeared into the what's-it, where I couldn't follow her. I couldn't very well wait outside either, so I went back and finished my breakfast.

At ten she went out. Again I followed. She walked at the most tremendous rate and, just at the crossroads, caught a bus. I tore after it, but it picked up too much speed and I couldn't make it.

Again not knowing what to do, I thumbed the next car, got a lift, and told the driver I wanted to go the same way as the bus. Luckily there was only one road, and this we followed. We got ahead of the bus and I waited at the terminus, about seven miles from Blaneden.

No Cassock. She must have got off that bus almost as soon as she got on, and I'd missed seeing her as the car whizzed onwards. I got the bus back to the town to find some of the townspeople in a terrific flap. It appeared that she was up on top of the cathedral tower screaming and

pointing and threatening to jump. It was then a quarter
past eleven, so she must have been up there some time.

Half the town had arrived by the time I got there, and
the fire brigade had been sent for. One or two of our party
were there, and young Robert Binns dashed ahead of me
and went up the steps like a cat. I put my best foot forward
but was nothing like so quick. These newel staircases have
treads too narrow for feet as big as mine. When I got on to
the leads—it meant climbing two rickety ladders after
we'd reached the bells—the kid was gripping her with both
arms round her waist and she was battering his head with
her fists, and they were swaying about like two wrestlers
almost up to the parapet (which wasn't any too high).

I seized her wrists and told the kid to let go. She fought
like hell at first, and then went quiet and apologized for
being a nuisance, but I didn't feel I could trust her enough
to let go. I said to the kid, 'Don't look,' but, of course, he
did. I clipped her a short jab under the jaw and laid her
out. Then I told young Robert to get down the first ladder
and hold it, and I slung her over my shoulder and made
for the opening. The fun began, of course, when I discovered that the trap-door down from the roof wouldn't
take the two of us at once, so I had to wait until she came
to, and then I went down first and guided her feet. She
was sobbing by the time we reached *terra firma*, having
scuffled the whole way down on her hands and knees. The
kid was grand, although, I think, badly scared. So was I.
Scared, I mean. I don't know whether she *would* have
chucked herself over—probably not—but at the first
opportunity I'm going to give that boy a present, because
I couldn't have got up there half as quickly as he did, and

it would have been a nice thing to have had to report a
suicide on the trip.

But I feel weak. Passengers like the Cassock are just a
shade over the odds. Anyway, everything went as right as
rain on the excursion this afternoon. We had the most
marvellous run. Went from here to Crieff and out along
Loch Earn to Lochearnhead and Killin. We came back
along the shore of Loch Tay to Aberfeldy, and from there
it was the most magnificent scenery imaginable—tremendous gorges, waterfalls, mountain views, more lochs
(small ones), and a wonderful sight of Schiehallion, a
mountain I've always wanted to see.

This morning we left immediately after breakfast for
the Devil's Elbow, Braemar, and Balmoral. Finding that
I was a bit put out about the sea trip, before he
went Parks apologized, but said that his wife didn't like
the idea of tackling the Devil's Elbow pass in a motor-
coach. They went yesterday, after dinner. Oh, I told
you.

This Devil's Elbow, it seems, is part of the highest road
in the British Isles (1,950 feet, leading on to the Cairnwell
Pass at 2,199 feet), and has some very awkward bends
which bring Mrs. Parks' heart into her mouth whenever
she thinks of them.

I accepted this explanation (which I don't believe,
because I simply can't imagine Mrs. Parks being coy about
any road on earth, let alone one in her own country), but
I said I'd wished he'd told me before we left London so
that my owners could have O.K.-ed the scheme before he
actually got around to it.

Anyway, I shall have to count the flock and check up, as

I don't know at present who went off with him last evening. I was in the ballroom when they went.

We had a troupe of little girls doing Highland dances. Sweet kids they were, too; awfully pretty, and the dancing was first class, and it was while they were performing that Parks and his jolly sailor-boys-and-girls (heaven send them all such belly-wobbles on the rolling deep as'll make them wish they'd never sold their little farms and gone to sea!) went off to catch the night tide.

Just to add to the gaiety of nations, Bert thinks he's sprained his back, so, in the absence of the boat party, who might have given me a hand, I've had all the loading up to do this morning! I don't know what we shall do on the Devil's Elbow! *I* can't take the coach up and over it, and I don't see how Bert's going to cope, if his back is as bad as he says it is.

[15]

We're in Aberdeen a couple of nights, which should give the sailors time to catch up with us before we leave for Inverness. Parks has left me with twenty-one passengers and, of course, Bert. His back got all right, by the way.

I've checked up on Parks' amateur crew. He's taken the two Peels, Miss Pratt (thank God!), old Uncle Togg, Mrs. Hocking and Mrs. Amesby (silly old trollops!), Miss Cann (to get away from Mrs. Cassock, I shouldn't wonder), and his wife. Nine in all, counting him. And I thought he said half a dozen at most—in other words, six others, himself and his wife, making eight in all. I should have thought that a pretty fair number. Don't see how he could possibly sleep anyone else. It's his look out, of course, but he told me distinctly that six besides themselves was the fullest possible crew. I'm glad he's got the Pratt. Serve him right!

The Devil's Elbow turned out to be a glorious brute of a road. We came up to it after we'd left Spittal of Glenshee. The hairpins are really wicked. I don't think I could have tackled Bert's job of getting our big bus round them, but the scenery was superb, and so were some rough-haired collies handling a large flock of sheep. The Pratt, had she been with us (which, thank goodness, she wasn't) would have found plenty of work for that ciné-camera of hers.

[16]

Went to the sea early this morning. Walked. It seemed miles upon miles upon miles, and a lot of it definitely slummy. Discovered I could have ridden on a tram for a penny! Yes, they have penny fares in Aberdeen.

The sea was very grey, and when I got to the beach (which I did by walking under a sort of primitive archway) I saw salmon fishers. There were five of them in a heavy rowing boat. They were silhouetted black—just shapes, but good ones—against the rising sun. It was rather marvellous.

Bathing was very good indeed, the water as cold as it looked, and I raced for a tram coming back, feeling fresh as a daisy. No sign of Parks and the others at breakfast, but I'm no longer worrying. I don't care if it rains Parks and Pratts to-morrow all day long.

I am sorry to say that poor Wrenn became very much off-colour again, and his wife managed to persuade him to give up the tour. I think he'd only stuck it out as long as he did so as not to spoil her holiday. I didn't see him before we left as he was asleep after a very bad night. I managed to get them a room at a reasonable rate at Blaneden—the management were awfully good—and they'll go home from there when he's fit enough.

To add to my troubles there seems a bit of a mystery about Parks' passengers and crew. According to my checking there should have been nine of them on the boat, including Parks himself, but he could only account for eight when he got back. He swears that Miss Pratt was not one of the ones who opted for the cruise, and he has no knowledge at all of where she is. He added, too, that he told me at the time that he couldn't have more than eight on board, and, of course, that's quite correct—he did tell me.

Damn! This means I've got to telephone the hotel at Blaneden, where, presumably, the confounded woman is marooned. I suppose she went out by herself and didn't get back, or something. Quite a number of people seem to lose all their sense of responsibility when they're on holiday, and I suppose she's one of them.

[17]

I'm rather worried. Miss Nordle, who 'goes with' Miss Pratt, has confided to me what I'd more or less gathered before, that they *did* have a row at Blaneden—apparently a pretty bad one—and that when Pratt didn't turn up on the coach she supposed she'd gone off in a pet and joined

Parks' crew, which, after all, was the natural thing to think, I suppose. It's what I also thought she'd done, although I wasn't considering the row.

Anyhow, the joke (I don't think!) is that I've telephoned Blaneden and the management haven't a clue. None of the party was left behind, they say, except the Wrenns, and all the baggage was collected. This proves to be true, because the Pratt baggage was on the coach. I didn't remember loading it on—you remember Bert had a kink in his back—so I queried their statement, and then they said that a chambermaid had come running down with it after the loading-up was done, and a hotel porter shoved it in the boot. Of course, I didn't do the unloading at this end because Bert's back was all right by then, and I wasn't even present, because I was checking in at the hotel office and getting keys and things.

I don't know what to make of it so I've sent a telegram to Pratt's address to ask her people to notify me at Inverness if she's gone home. But would she go home without her luggage?

On second thoughts, I'll put a call through to Mrs. Wrenn. As she's staying at Blaneden she may know something about her. Pity I didn't think of that before I sent to London.

[18]

Talk about 'would it were bedtime and all were well!'— it's bedtime all right, and that's as far as I can go. The Wrenns—it was a shame to have bothered them really— don't know a thing about Pratt, and now, after dinner,

Miss Nordle comes to me just as I'm about to shepherd
the mob to the Beach Pavilion (which they could find
perfectly well on their own, but they won't be bothered)
and confides that when she and the Pratt had this row at
Blaneden, 'Lilias spoke and acted very strangely,' and she's
'afraid she may have done something to herself, she's so
temperamental.'

I don't believe she's anything like temperamental
enough to deprive us of her charming company by committing suicide, but I didn't say so; I merely soothed the
wretched female and gave it as my opinion (which it is)
that she was probably all upset and took herself off home
without a word to any of us.

I'm thankful in a way to be quit of her. She's a bit too
nymphomaniac for my liking. I told you that before, but
I haven't told you that even old Togg has complained.
Says she makes him go gooseflesh. She certainly does *me*.
Bert has a word for her. It's unprintable and most fear-
fully, wonderfully apt! All the same, I do wish she hadn't
hopped it like this, without a word. It messes up the tour
and the Nordle goes about looking like a self-accused
criminal. I don't like her, but I wouldn't mind betting
that Pratt is much the more pernicious of the two. Incidentally, Parks doesn't think we need worry about Pratt.
He says little tarantulas live where big elephants die.

[19]

Still no news of the Pratt, but we're here in Inverness
until Monday morning. I forgot to tell you that Mrs.

Cassock—who seems normal again in most respects, although she has taken to smoking a pipe as she can't get enough cigarettes—resolutely refused to see a doctor in Aberdeen, and we could think of no way to lead her to it. Miss Nordle looks as though she's going to be ill. I suppose she must have a kind heart, really, but I wish she wouldn't keep coming to me and bleating that it's all her fault that poor Lilias is missing half this lovely holiday. It's wearing.

I've heard again from the Wrenns. They've managed to book a sleeper and are going home on Monday. It *is* rotten. It's costing them a lot of money to have a perfectly foul time, and they're decent people.

But I'm getting wretchedly worried about Miss Pratt, too. I can't help feeling that she isn't, after all, the type to have gone back home in a huff. She didn't seem the kind who would spend her money and then lose half the fun. I only hope she hasn't got mixed up in some unpleasant way with one of the local lads. She's the type to boggle at nothing if it came in a kilt or long trews. I wonder she hasn't bought it long ago! It isn't for want of persistence. All the men on this bus can swear to that! Even young Robert!

Talking of Robert, I ought to detail what happened at Elgin Cathedral. Robert contrived, while the rest of us were dutifully following the guide towards the Chapter House, to get the door open to one of the west towers. The next we saw of him was a balancing feat across a sort of gallery about sixty feet above the ground from which he waved to us.

I said that the Cassock had been well-behaved, but she threw some sort of fit at seeing Robert up there and bolted back to inform Parks and myself that Robert had seen them kill her baby. Parks thought it was horrid ghoulish, and ordered Robert to come down.

Personally, I think she was pulling a stunt. There's some story of a mad woman who, in 1748, used the piscina as a cradle for her infant. The baby was a boy, and when he grew up he enlisted in the service of the Honourable East India Company and rose to the rank of Lieutenant-General. Like most of the nabobs of the time, he amassed a considerable fortune, but, unlike the majority, he bequeathed quite a bit to the town of Elgin, and is, I believe, revered and respected to this day.

Anyway, we coaxed the Cassock out into the open on the pretence of looking for the baby, and from the nave—now open to the sky and pleasantly turfed—we got her back to the coach, Parks wiping his brow and me feeling that at Inverness she was going to see a doctor whether she liked it or not. The rest of the party tactfully looked at—and some bought—picture postcards while we, assisted by Parks' missus and Mrs. Wells, got our bird safely stowed and soothed. But the incident wasn't funny; it was embarrassing, for one thing, and rather alarming for another.

We got to Inverness in good time, and there are no complaints up to date about the allotment of the rooms. Miss Pew has bought herself a tartan scarf (Clan Macleod, which is brightish with a lot of yellow in it), and old Leese, not to be outdone, has invested in a Glengarry in which he looks like Bill Sykes' elder brother. The various ladies are embellished with hare's-foot brooches, clan badges, to which, needless to say, they're not entitled, enamel and silver thistles, cairngorms, and, in the case of Miss Nordle, a gosh-awful coat-ornament consisting of two quite noticeably large silver tassies, one bearing the legend 'A Wee Deoch,' the other 'an Doris.' The enquiring and embarrassing Durdle, poor old soul, asked me to explain who Deoch and Doris were! *Could* she have been pulling my leg? She's been rather well informed up to now.

[20]

Left Inverness at nine and have had a real Highland day. That is to say, it has poured with rain from morning to night. That's not quite true, either, because it was still fine at Carrbridge, where we had morning coffee. The old bridge there is well worth seeing. Our camera party photographed it, needless to say, and Miss Nordle openly deplored the fact that the ciné-camera was no longer with us. A piper, followed by half a dozen kids, went past the hotel, and I think that's what the Nordle was keenest on, although she proffered the opinion that the bridge was 'quite, quite twee.' I'm finding it awfully difficult to get her off my neck. She seems to think we are partners in distress (or, possibly, crime) over the absence of the Pratt. Nevertheless, she's become quite cheerful again.

[21]

We're in a spot. Miss Pratt's body was found on that boat Parks hired. The police have been here at Lakewater

since ten, and it's going to be sticky. It's no good saying
I'm not going to worry. I'm worried stiff. I don't know
what to expect, but I do know, before the police tell me,
that somebody on the tour knows something about what's
happened. The news blew up first thing this morning.

By the way (and I hate to ask you this), I suppose you
couldn't interest your old lady in our spot of bother? . . . I
don't see why you should be able to, but . . . could you?
I don't see my way clear, and she's reputed to be a marvel.
Only one thing seems clear so far. They're building up the
details of the last day the poor wretched woman was
known to be alive, and it's obvious to me already that she
was most probably killed before we left Blaneden. How
the body got on to the boat is still anybody's guess, but
there's no doubt the police are pretty certain that one or
more of our coach party must be suspected. As we're all
from the London area, and the confounded boat has a
Thames registration, I imagine the Yard will take over
but even that isn't settled yet, because the dreadful business actually took place in Scotland. We may all be taken
back to Blaneden for questioning. It seems pretty clear she
died on the Wednesday, but at what time we don't yet
know. There's only one clue, so far. A piece of paper was
found rolled up in the rug in which the body was wrapped.
Printed on it in red pencil were the words: *The Devil gives
the elbow to such as this.* But for contempt of court or whatever it is, I'd put my shirt on Mrs. Cassock, but it isn't fair
to say so, I suppose.

Mrs. Lestrange Bradley turned up like a sulphurous angel yesterday afternoon, having motored from London, driven by her chauffeur George, at about the pace by which Lucifer fell from heaven. Sorry for all the brimstone references, but she makes me feel like that. She brought Scotland Yard with her (unofficially at present . . . he is on leave). In fact, the particular inspector she's got turns out to be the prospective husband of that same Laura Menzies whose place you are filling, darling Em, while she is on holiday. Thanks be. What luck, isn't it? I trust the old lady absolutely to see us through, especially as in charge of the case at present is a *very* raw-boned Caledonian named Inspector Ian Mactavish, who has already made up his mind, I think, that *I* done it!

BOOK TWO

Mrs. Bradley's Conversations

*

'*Now we come to Scotland . . .*'
Charles Dickens: *A Child's History of England*

'*The state of man does change and vary,*
Now sound, now sick, now blyth, now sary,
Now dansand mirry, nor like to die:—
Timor mortis conturbat me.'
William Dunbar: *Lament for the Makers*

'SO THERE IT IS,' said Mrs. Bradley. She was sitting in an armchair in the private suite she had taken at the 'Scottish Lion,' Blaneden, looking less like a sulphurous angel than like a small, thin, energetic spider interviewing diffident flies. 'I'll see Mr. Jeffries first.'

Her victim was a dark-haired, blue-eyed young man of loose, athletic build and with unusually long legs. He had, in addition, the pleasantly unkempt appearance associated by her with nephews of whom she approved. In other words and, in general, Mr. George Hugh Jeffries had much in common with her more attractive young relatives, and possessed, so far as she could make out on such slight acquaintance, every one of their virtues and almost none of their faults.

She took as great a fancy to him, in fact, as she had taken, a fortnight or so before, to his green-eyed, smooth-

cheeked Em, and Mr. Jeffries, instinctively appropriating
her affections, as is the way of young men with old
ladies, felt considerably more comforted than, under the
circumstances in which he found himself, he would have
believed to be possible, and he answered her questions
forthrightly (and without those pauses into which, rightly
or wrongly, a psychologist reads so much) in a clear but
gentle voice.

'Yes,' he was saying, 'that's how it was, you see, and I
think that's every syllable I know.'

Mrs. Bradley, remembering his letters to Em, nodded in
complete agreement. She knew that it was everything he
thought he knew. She felt certain, moreover, that before
her was an innocent man, for the indiscreet references in
the letters to his difficulties and to his likes and dislikes, his
observations on murder, and his crude but helpful character sketches of his coach party, would have been
sufficiently revealing of his innocence without the added
evidence supplied by his appearance, his conversation, and
his well-balanced, modest personality.

Mrs. Bradley, in short, decided to wipe her Em's Dan
Chaucer once and for all off her list of suspects. She already
had said as much over the house telephone to her partner
and co-operator, Detective-Inspector Gavin, and to
Inspector Mactavish of the Perthshire police.

She and Gavin were working together on the case, but
Gavin so far had no official standing. He was on leave from
the Yard, and his status at the moment was that of Mrs.
Bradley's friend. She herself held the accredited position
of consulting psychologist to the Home Office. She was
also there in her ex-mural capacity of Em's temporary boss,

but this did not appear in the minutes and was of no interest to anybody except Jeffries. Mactavish, to his credit, had welcomed her warmly.

The adorable Em had gone to Mrs. Bradley in tears, and Em in tears was sufficient to melt the snows on Everest, let alone the tender heart which Mrs. Bradley retained especially for the young of both sexes bedevilled and besotted with love.

'Of course I'll go along and help,' Mrs. Bradley had said. 'Now just you tell me everything you know.'

So Em had produced the letters, a fact with which Jeffries, fortunately for his peace of mind, was, so far, unacquainted.

'Now, Mr. Jeffries,' Mrs. Bradley went on, after he had said that he thought he knew no more, 'there are one or two further questions I should like to put to you.'

'I don't think . . .' the young man began, but Mrs. Bradley was having none of that.

'I know you don't think you know anything more than you've told me,' she observed, 'but there are matters on which I should like to have some footnotes. Here at Blaneden, for example, you went out for early morning walks. Now, when you took an early walk on the Tuesday, the day after your arrival, you described it in some detail. Do you remember?—the pine wood, the squirrel, the rabbits, the caravan, the hare, how you lost yourself and listened for the sound of the burn——?'

'You haven't read all that muck I wrote to Em?' said Jeffries, aghast.

'Of course I have. Have you ever thought of writing novels, Mr. Jeffries?'

'Well, yes, of course. I mean, most people do, but . . .'

'I think there is a future for you in authorship. But that is beside the question for the moment. My point is this: as you took such pains to describe *that* walk, why did you pass over the *next* walk, the one you took on the Wednesday morning—the morning of the day on which Miss Pratt was killed?'

'Oh, I don't know! I say! You *must* think me a fool! Those letters were only scribbled off just for Em, you know. She likes to read a lot of rot. I never thought anybody else . . .'

Mrs. Bradley cackled.

'Em's likes may have saved you a great deal of trouble, including several hours of Scottish police questioning,' she remarked. 'Cheer up, child, and answer the question.'

'I can't. I don't know why I didn't describe the second walk. I suppose I didn't think it would interest Em.'

'Where did your five miles take you?'

'Oh, up the long hill behind the hotel, and through the farm, and up on to the high moors. I stepped it out pretty fast, because I went chiefly for exercise, and I suppose that's why I didn't really notice a lot.'

'I gathered as much. Did you see any of your coach party?'

'No.'

'Anybody at the farm?'

'Yes, one man. He told me the way to take.'

'Through the farmyard?'

'Yes. Apparently there's a right of way. At any rate, they let people through. And the dog that had barked before was a long-haired collie.'

'Was the motor-caravan still in the field by the stone wall?'

'Yes, but there was nobody about.'

'Not on the return journey either?'

'I don't know. I found another way to come back, so I didn't see the caravan again.'

'When did you last see Miss Pratt alive?'

'I've been trying to remember. I'm not at all sure that I can say. I mean, I know I saw her at dinner on the previous night, but . . .'

'Wait a minute. Let's make a timetable,' said Mrs. Bradley, turning to a fresh leaf in her notebook. 'You set out from London with your party on the Thursday and reached Arrowbridge the same evening. You left Arrowbridge on the Friday morning and stayed Friday night, Saturday night and Sunday night at Scotstone, across the Border. You left Scotstone for Blaneden, and stayed here Monday night, all day Tuesday and all day Wednesday. At some time on Wednesday Miss Pratt was killed. You saw her at dinner on Tuesday night, but not on Wednesday night. . . .'

'But she must have been in to dinner on Wednesday night, you know. She'd have been missed. The boat party didn't leave until dinner was over. I do know that for a fact.'

'Ah, now we begin to see the pattern which our inquiry will have to take. Mr. Jeffries, please try to visualize the party at dinner on that Wednesday night. With whom did you sit at table?'

'Oh, with Miss Baird, Miss Carter, the two Parks and, of course, old Leese.'

'How were the other tables made up?'

'I don't think I can remember. The two Miss Tooleys were with the Viccars couple, and at the same table were Togg and his niece, Miss Macklin; that makes two sixes—twelve in all. Then there were the two Peels, Miss Bernard, Miss Moxon, Mrs. Hocking and Mrs. Amesby at another table, and at the next table were, I think, the three Wells, Miss Cann, Miss Durdle and . . .yes, and Miss Nordle. . . .'

'The quarrel between Miss Pratt and Miss Nordle having already taken place . . . yes?'

'Then there were Miss Pew, Mrs. Adderley, old Mrs. Binns and young Robert Binns . . . how many is that? Oh, and of course—no, that's right.'

'Twenty-eight, that comes to.'

'Hm! Four unaccounted for. One was Mrs. Cassock . . . she'd already said she wasn't coming down, so I had a tray sent up.'

'Did she eat her dinner?'

'I've no idea, I'm afraid. I know I was charged an extra bob on the bill, and so I was for the Wrenns, who also had trays sent up. Wrenn was feeling particularly seedy that evening. As I suppose you know, he didn't come any further than Blaneden, and they're back in London now. Do you know, it almost seems as though Miss Pratt *wasn't* in for dinner that night.'

'Yes, we may assume that, I think. But we can easily find out. Someone may have inquired after her, but, even if nobody did, Miss Nordle will know. Of course, if Miss Pratt was not at dinner, Miss Nordle probably thought that Miss Pratt was piqued as a result of the quarrel, and was staying upstairs in her room instead of coming down to the meal, so she may not have commented on her absence; but she'll *know*.'

'That's about the size of it. It doesn't help much in establishing the time of death, though, except that, as the police doctor said, it must have taken place on that Wednesday.'

'We can go a little farther. Did Miss Pratt go on the outing to Crieff and Killin?'

'No, she didn't. I've got a list somewhere of the people who did go. I have to keep lists because I pay all the bills for outings, and get the money back from the party afterwards.'

He took a loose-leaf notebook out of a despatch case and found the list he wanted. He handed it over. Miss Pratt's name was not on it. Mrs. Bradley copied the names that were there, and compared this list with the full list of passengers which she had compiled from his letters to Em.

'I see,' she said, 'that Miss Pratt, Mr. and Mrs. Parks, Mr. and Mrs. Wrenn, Miss Macklin and Miss Durdle did not go.'

'As a matter of fact, Miss Durdle *did* go,' said Jeffries. He blushed and grinned. 'She said she couldn't afford another outing. She had gone on the one to the Trossachs and Loch Katrine the day before, you see, and she said she couldn't manage the Killin trip, so . . . well, I . . .'

'Yes, I see,' said Mrs. Bradley. 'That was nice, Dan. Please put her name on the list. It will make things easier for the police when they impound your collection of documents.' Jeffries added Miss Durdle's name and received a kindly and approving pat on the back from Mrs. Bradley.

'I see that Miss Nordle went with you,' she continued, 'but that neither Miss Pratt nor Miss Nordle went on the previous outing, so I presume that the quarrel took place during Tuesday when, in all probability, they had gone out together.'

'I've an idea that they'd had a bit of a bust before that.'

'Indeed?'

'Yes. I didn't think they seemed too matey when they came back from their personal trip to Edinburgh. The one they took from Scotstone, if you remember. I expect you've gathered what I thought of them, but all that fearful heartiness about what fun they'd had in Edinburgh with the ciné-camera, and so forth, didn't ring true, somehow. I mean, they *were* shockingly hearty, always, but this didn't seem quite their usual style. Of course, I've really nothing to go on, and I said practically nothing to Em in the letter, but that's when I think it all began. We had to put up with a fearful amount of girlishness that evening, but I think they were sort of scoring off each other all the time.'

'Interesting,' said Mrs. Bradley. 'You have made a most valuable suggestion. I shall certainly bear it in mind. I should like to see a list, at some time, of those who went on the outing to Lanark.'

She made this statement with such a leer upon her yellow countenance that Jeffries flinched as though he had trodden on a snake. The reptilian old lady received this reaction with a hoot of sardonic laughter, and poked him in the ribs with a wicked forefinger.

'If . . . if anything else occurs to me, I'll let you know,' said Jeffries nervously. 'As for Lanark, everybody went except Pratt, Nordle, Durdle, Parkses, Peels, and Pew. Oh, and Bert, of course.'

'Good. And thank you very much, Mr. Jeffries, for your ready co-operation.' Mrs. Bradley uttered this banality in her usual beautiful voice. 'When you go away, will you please ask Mr. Peel to see me?'

Jeffries went out at once and, after a short pause, Mr. Peel came in. This gentleman had the general demeanour of a rat. He was thin, tough, quick-eyed, sharp-nosed and furtively aggressive. He was also beautifully dressed, but this did nothing to qualify Mrs. Bradley's first unfavourable impression. If anything, it somewhat heightened it.

'I should wish to know your authority for questioning me,' he said. Mrs. Bradley produced a stupefying portfolio full of documents and handed it to him without a word. He turned over the top two or three papers, handed the portfolio back, and, leaning back in his chair, said, 'Well, I've nothing to hide, and the sooner we get to the bottom of the business the sooner we'll all get home, I imagine. Fire away.'

He then clasped his hands behind his head, stretched his feet out, crossed them, and closed his wary little eyes.

'I would rather tell you our difficulty before I ask for your help,' said Mrs. Bradley. 'I was called into this case as a consulting psychologist, and I deduce (from my inspection of Miss Pratt's body) that this murder is much more likely to have been a man's crime than a woman's.'

'Why?'

'She was killed by a very heavy blow on the back of the head. Her skull was crushed.'

'Well, that lets out the coach party, then. Surely none of us went round with sandbags packed in our suitcases!'

'That is loose reasoning. A cosh is easily hidden. Are you arguing that a complete stranger murdered Miss Pratt?'

'I don't know who murdered her, but I should have thought that since the war there were plenty of killers about. One reads of such attacks every day.'

'You have missed one point, I think. Who, except a member of the coach party, would have thought of putting the body on that boat which Commander Parks chartered?'

'Couldn't that have been coincidence?'

'It could, of course, but surely the body would have been more easily hidden on a larger craft?'

'What I can't understand,' said Peel, in a dreamy tone which was calculated to be irritating to the listener, 'was what benefit the person thought would come of moving the body at all. So much more sensible to have left her where she was, after robbing her of her handbag. No one would have thought of the coach party then, and none of us need have been bothered. It was *certainly* a thug, I tell you!'

Mrs. Bradley nodded. Mr. Peel did not lack brains, she decided, nor a sense of his own danger. There were very few men in the coach party. He was one of them.

'Why did you go on the trip to Crieff and Killin?' she asked suddenly.

'Why? Well, to . . . just to take the trip, I suppose. Why shouldn't I have taken it?'

'No reason at all. Did you go on the previous day to the Trossachs and Loch Katrine?'

'No. I went with Parks to Leith to see about this beastly boat of his. Girlie . . . my wife, you know . . . went to the Trossachs. I wished I'd gone when she told me about it. I had a thoroughly messy, boring time, and she seems to have had quite a good one.'

'Yes. Who were the caravanners?'

'Oh, those people camping on the rise behind this hotel, you mean? I haven't the faintest idea. Parks and I went out for a before-breakfast stroll, don't you know, and saw the people, and passed the time of day. Who told you we talked to them? Nobody else was about.'

'You are mistaken. There was one person in the pine woods and another in the lane. Both were members of the coach party.'

'Oh, I see. Some of these women are born snoopers and gossips. Anyway, it doesn't matter who saw us, does it? The chap seemed a nice fellow, and the wife was charming. They gave us a whole lot of dope . . . history and so forth, you know . . . about the locality. Very interesting indeed.' He eyed her warily.

'Ah, yes. Did you see them on the following day?'

'On the Wednesday? No. They'd gone. But you surely don't suspect . . .? They weren't the type to—I mean, they were quite all right in every way. Just upper middle-class people like ourselves.'

'I thought a caravan might be a convenient means of transport for a corpse,' explained Mrs. Bradley, leering at her upper middle-class victim with carnivorous affection.

'Oh, but . . . I mean, why should they?'

'I don't know. Thank you, Mr. Peel. What did you do when the local coach took a party out to Lanark?'

'Lanark? When was that? . . . Oh yes, I remember. Boring, I thought. I went fishing.'

'And your wife?'

'Girlie? Oh, the Parkses took her to Peebles.'

'I don't think I need trouble Mrs. Peel at present, then. I am sure you have told me everything I wanted to know.'

'Charmed.'

'If you would be so good as to send in Mrs. Cassock,' said Mrs. Bradley.

'That pestilence? You won't get anything useful out of her. She's completely mad, and should never have been allowed to come on the trip.'

'I entirely agree. But will you please ask her to come and see me?'

Mrs. Cassock came without delay.

'And I did, did, did, did, *did* jump off the tower,' she remarked. 'It was as high in the sky as a pie. Is a pie high? It depends on the liver. Like living long. Long John Silver was a character in *As You Like It*. Why wasn't he? Don't tell me.'

'I shouldn't dream of telling you,' said Mrs. Bradley. '*You* tell *me*.'

'It was not so shocking,' said Mrs. Cassock. 'You see, he didn't really mean it. I always think that makes such a difference, don't you?'

'I certainly agree. And if he didn't mean it, who did?'

'Ah, *that!*' said Mrs. Cassock, with a cunning gleam in an otherwise fishlike eye. 'That was Annabel Lee.'

'A gipsy?'

'Oh, yes. Amyas Leigh and Gipsy Lee and George Borrow. One should never borrow. Loan oft loses both itself and friend. Lone, lone, lone. Lone in the depths of the sea. And we loved with a love that was more than love, I and my Annabel Lee, and I didn't mean to kill her. Baby said, "Hit him on the head, bang." He didn't mean it.'

'But Annabel Lee didn't live in a caravan,' Mrs. Bradley pointed out.

'No, it was too, too cynical. No, I don't mean cynical. What do I mean? Are *you* mean? I should have thought you were a generous person. Generous generation upon generous generation, and Abraham begat Isaac. Who told you?'

'You did, of course,' said Mrs. Bradley. 'Don't you remember? All those people in caravans, and the pine trees sighing and dying.'

'Sighing and dying. Dying. Dying. They dyed my dress green. I never liked it. Would *you* have liked it?'

'It's the gipsy's choice. That, and red.'

> 'Blood is red, steel is blue,
> Men are hell, and so are you,'

said Mrs. Cassock rapidly, blinking her codfish eyes. Mrs. Bradley added to her notebook some data upon word-associations and the dangers of a literary education, then she gave Mrs. Cassock a bag of sweets, and told her to sit on the settee and eat them. Within ten minutes Mrs. Cassock, who wore the contented expression of somebody who had got something off her mind, was apparently fast asleep.

Mrs. Bradley studied her; then, none too gently, she made a dart at her and had the interesting experience of seeing her flinch.

'No!' exclaimed Mrs. Cassock, sitting up. 'I'll tell you! Don't hurt me. He was always so violent. He hit me on the head. That was what he did. And I saw—what did I see? My daughter and my ducats. I think I . . .'

This time, no doubt of it, she fell asleep.

'She has unburdened herself of something,' said Mrs. Bradley to Detective Inspector Gavin, 'and if what she has told me is true, it should help us considerably.' She studied her notes of Mrs. Cassock's evidence. 'She is certainly trying to tell us that she saw the murder committed. What do you think about that?'

'The puir wifie havers,' said Inspector Mactavish compassionately. Mrs. Bradley could not help wondering whether the reference was to herself or Mrs. Cassock, for the inspector's eye was unfathomable. She shrugged, and sent Gavin for Miss Nordle. Miss Nordle looked ill. She had not slept, she said, since the accident to poor Lilias. She did not think, she said, that she would ever sleep properly again. She said that she dreaded the *dark*. She added that one *never knew*, did one?

Mrs. Bradley added sympathetic comments; then she asked with extreme suddenness:

'And what are you afraid of, Miss Nordle? . . . being hanged?'

Miss Nordle, after a protesting gasp at the nakedness of the question, said that no, no, of course it was not that, but she *did* wonder whether anything might be going to happen to *her*.

'Why should it?' asked Mrs. Bradley.

'Well, it happened to Lilias,' replied Miss Nordle, 'and we were very close friends.'

'You mean the ciné-camera,' said Mrs. Bradley in such conclusive tones that Miss Nordle gasped again. 'Come along, Miss Nordle. What about the ciné-camera? What did you two quarrel about in Edinburgh?'

Miss Nordle gave a slight moan.

'But we *didn't!*' she said. 'We didn't really quarrel *at all!* It was only that . . . one should not speak ill of the dead . . . but it was . . . well, you see, Lilias was, should I say, tipsy while we were in Edinburgh? No, no, I won't. It wasn't as bad as that. But we had . . .' she gave a repulsive little giggle, '. . . well, as a matter of fact, we *did* have a wee dock and then, of course, a weeny little Doris.'

Detective-Inspector Gavin, whose birthplace had been far north of the Tweed, gave a smothered snort of laughter and then an apologetic cough to cover it up. He did not catch Inspector Mactavish's eye.

'Deoch-an-doris,' he said gently.

'That's what I said,' protested Miss Nordle. 'And what I said at the time was that Lilias shouldn't have had them. She knew it always affected her. Even at Christmas time she couldn't take anything without coming over all silly, especially two whisky-ports, which is what we had.'

'What's a whisky-port?' asked Gavin.

'Oh, don't you know? I thought all gentlemen knew about drinks, quite different to poor little innocent me! Well, you know a *brandy*-port, I suppose? Well, this was a *whisky*-port. It's a pick me-up. It was after we had them

C

and then the beer which the gentleman treated us to, that Lilias got the idea of taking the picture of the other gentleman, the one in the tartan trousers.'

'What other gentleman was this?'

'Well, I don't know, really, and I did tell Lilias she ought not to do it without him knowing, but she had wound off quite a spool of him before he realized, and when he realized he was unpleasant. I don't mean really threatening, but not pleasant. He said she should ought to have got *permission* before she used a ciné-camera in public, and, of course, that's what I'd been telling her all the time.'

'But he did not use threatening language?' Gavin inquired.

'Oh, well, he did, in a way. He said he would throw the camera down and *jump* on it.'

'And after that?'

'There wasn't much after that,' said Miss Nordle in a tone of regret. 'I acted lady-like, and walked off, and left Lilias to follow. We were attracting attention, you see.'

'And where is the ciné-camera now?'

'But that's what I'm *telling* you! That's why I'm so frightened and worried. It isn't *anywhere!* You see, Lilias *had* it—well, it belonged to her, of course——'

'And what you really quarrelled about was Miss Pratt's behaviour in public after she had had these drinks?'

'It *began* with that,' said Miss Nordle, abandoning the ciné-camera and seizing upon the subject offered in its place, 'but you know how things go when we girls start arguing. I know I mustn't speak ill of the dead, but, after all—and, besides, I don't think Lilias need have spoken as she did about me and Mr. Jeffries.'

'What did she say about you and Mr. Jeffries?' asked Gavin, with a good deal of interest. Miss Nordle pursed her lips and wriggled expressively, but Mrs. Bradley, still sitting back, clicked her tongue. This galvanized Miss Nordle into protecting herself.

'*Of course* there was nothing between Mr. Jeffries and I,' she affirmed, not at all to anyone's surprise. 'I mean, I should never consider—I mean, we only *met* on this tour, and, after all, one has other interests—I mean——'

'And Mr. Jeffries has only one other interest,' said Mrs. Bradley, 'so perhaps we should leave it at that.'

'Well, I can't help being more . . . well . . . *enivrée* with gentlemen than Lilias was,' explained Miss Nordle, 'although, as I had to point out, I can and do behave with them, and, of course, it taking her the way it did, she wished to be just *nasty*, and, well, of course, there were *words*, that's all.'

'Now, Miss Nordle, I would like you to think very carefully before you answer my next question,' said Gavin, leaning forward impressively. 'When did you last see Miss Pratt alive?'

Miss Nordle had evidently been expecting this question, a fact which Mrs. Bradley was inclined to think was a pity.

'I *think*,' she said, 'it would have been at the Wednesday breakfast.'

'Surely you know?' suggested Gavin, putting on a wolf-smile for her benefit.

'Well, *actually*,' said Miss Nordle, obviously *enivrée* with this particular gentleman, 'you see, I'd hardly know, it being my first day, and I inclined to a black-out. I remember saying to Lilias before dinner on the Tuesday that we should go and look over the cathedral next day, thinking I could have a nice sit-down in there, and it being one of the objects of interest in Blaneden which you're sort of always expected to go and see, there being a man where I work which is rather superior in education and that, and I thought it would make a nice subject of conversation, but she wouldn't, not being keen at all on churches, so I said to her what about a nice sundae, I having seen a shop which looked nice and clean, but she wouldn't take up with that either, so *words* began, and I felt I couldn't eat a thing at dinner, feeling all sick and that, and I hadn't cared for the fish the day before, either, trout being what I call turgid, so there it was.'

'Miss Nordle last saw Miss Pratt before dinner on the evening of Tuesday . . .' muttered Gavin.

'Oh, well, no, that isn't right!' cried Miss Nordle, before he could write the words down. 'I *did* see her at dinner on the *Tuesday*. It was the next morning I *didn't* see her, if you know what I mean. She never came down to breakfast, not so far as I know. But, you see, I didn't trouble, not then, thinking she had a fit of the sulks with me.'

'Now, Miss Nordle, don't let us worry too much about this quarrel of yours for the moment. Girls will be girls, I suppose?' Miss Nordle rose willingly to what she supposed was a gallant remark, but she had no chance to reply, for Gavin immediately continued: 'How well did you know Miss Pratt? Were you—did you work at the same place, or something of that sort?—or did your families meet? What was the connection between you?'

'As to that,' replied Miss Nordle, 'well, actually, I didn't really know Lilias at all well. I mean, up to this holiday, I suppose we hadn't, well, more than hardly met, except at the tennis club.'

'And that last statement is a lie if ever I heard one,' said Gavin to Mrs. Bradley when Miss Nordle had left them. 'And just why should she lie about a thing like that?'

'Fear,' said Mrs. Bradley. 'But, of course, she may not be lying.'

'Fear? Fear of what?'

'Of the police, of scandal, and of being murdered.'

'But she's such an idiot! Who on earth would want to murder a chump like her?'

'The same person, possibly, as murdered Miss Pratt. I wonder what mischief they *did* get up to with that ciné-camera? And I wonder where they went on the Tuesday, and whom they met, and what the second quarrel really was about?'

'How did you hitch on to the idea that the ciné-camera might be at the root of the trouble?' Gavin inquired. Mrs. Bradley answered that she was not sure that it was at the root of the trouble.

'It's a verra likely thing, that, all the same,' observed Inspector Mactavish. 'A verra likely thing, I would say. Gin they snooped around wi' it and caught some sinfu' body unawares, I wouldna say but what it wouldna be a motive for her demise.'

'It was something Mrs. Cassock said which put the

ciné-camera into my mind,' said Mrs. Bradley. 'She used
the word "cynical," and I knew that she could not mean
it. That is all. And now we must see the Wrenns.'

Mr. Wrenn was still extremely ill. There was no doubt
about that, and there was no doubt, either, that he had
been ill for a considerable time. In other words, neither
Gavin nor Mrs. Bradley could conceive of him as a possible
murderer. They agreed, in fact, that they did not think
his state of health would have allowed him to track down
and bludgeon Miss Pratt, still less that it would have
allowed him to help to transport the body to the boat
and hide it there, whatever he might have had against
her.

'I suppose he *is* as ill as he looks?' said Gavin discon-
tentedly, when they had left the sick man and had pooled
their identical opinions.

'There is no doubt of it. His heart is very weak indeed.'

'I know. I agreed before, and I agree now. The only
thing is that I can't understand why his doctor should ever
have allowed him to go on a motor-coach tour. It was a
grave responsibility to take.'

'Perhaps his doctor had no voice in the matter. I should
think it was entirely the idea of the Wrenns themselves.'

'Well, at any rate, we can wipe him off the list of suspects. If he'd attempted to bean that poor girl he'd have
fallen dead of the effort.'

'He certainly would not have been capable of the
murder itself. Whether he could have been involved as an
accessory *in any way*, time alone will show.'

'Time, the great ally,' said Gavin. 'Anyway, back to Scotland we go, and tackle some more of the bunch. They're getting restive, I know, and I suppose, from the point of view of abstract justice, Mactavish ought not to hold them, but he doesn't want to let them disperse before he has to. What do *you* think?'

'That being on the spot is more likely to stimulate their memories than their home environment will do. Besides, there is Mactavish's convenience to consider, as the murder occurred in his district.'

'That's exactly what *I* think. So now for the . . . whom do you think?'

'Robert Binns, I rather fancy.'

'The wee laddie?'

'I doubt whether he would relish the description, but, yes, the wee laddie; in other, and, I feel, more apt and descriptive words, the intrepid mountaineer; the picklock; the inscrutable pioneer; the embryo architect. 'He walks in glory on the hills; we dalesmen envy him afar.' That's Robert, you know. A most unusual and gifted child.'

'You appear to have fallen heavily for the lad,' said Gavin, laughing. Mrs. Bradley nodded solemnly.

'The older I grow,' she replied, 'the more fully and completely I realize that Creation should have begun and ended with boys. Boys, except perhaps for the golden eagle, the common mugwort and the water-lily (all of which in some respects they resemble), are the only beings who have mastered the arts of the gods. Let us go, therefore, to Olympus, and have audience of one of these inimitable and preternaturally favoured beings.'

Gavin looked at her in deep distrust, but her yellow countenance was as bland as that of a Chinaman, and, for once, her black eyes were unfocused and looked into eternity, an eternity completely composed of boys.

Robert, admonished by his grandmother to be sure to tell the truth (an implied slur upon his honour which he received in dignified silence), rose politely when Gavin and Mrs. Bradley came in, and placed a chair for the latter.

'Now, Robert,' said Gavin, '(unless you prefer to be called Binns), you know who we are and what we're here for. You must answer our questions as exactly as you can, and . . .'

'Pardon me,' said Robert, who was small and thin for his age, and had the cat-like movements necessary, probably, for his exploits, 'but I cannot undertake to answer questions from the police except in the presence of my lawyer.'

'*What!*' said Gavin. He glanced at Mrs. Bradley, but she gave him no assistance. In fact, she undermined his little brief authority with an aunt-like and unrepentant chuckle. 'Well, but, look here, old chap, you haven't *got* a lawyer.' He boggled and continued helplessly, 'And, in any case, this is only an informal inquiry.'

'As a matter of fact, I *have* got a lawyer,' contradicted Robert. He picked up the house telephone and spoke to the hotel desk. 'Kindly ask Mr. MacKennon to come up to my grandmother's suite.'

Inspector Mactavish masked his emotions. Gavin

expired with faint oaths. Mrs. Bradley gazed at Robert with the transfixed ecstasy of a boa-constrictor considering the most expeditious method of seizing upon and swallowing its prey, and, in less than a minute, there was a gentle rap upon the door. In walked a black-coated, rubicund gentleman in his early forties, wearing (possibly for purposes of identification, but more probably because he was proud of it) a small clan badge on his lapel. He bowed, smiled, took a seat, produced an astonishingly large notebook apparently from beneath his waistcoat, and nodded in a friendly manner at Robert, taking no further notice of anybody else in the room.

'Noo juist ye go aheid, ma wee monnie,' he said, 'and when I say "Whist," ye'll haud your tongue.'

'You won't need to say that,' said Robert. 'Don't worry, MacKennon. I shall know. I'm just simply hazing these dicks.'

Mrs. Bradley thought this more than probable. She exchanged a crocodile grin for a non-committal tight smile from Inspector Mactavish.

'Now then, Robert,' she said, 'I want you to tell me at what time you got up in the morning on the day that Miss Pratt was killed.'

'At a quarter past five a.m.'

'Right. What did you do between a quarter past five and breakfast time?'

'I left the hotel and went for a walk.'

'Where did you go?'

'First I went uphill behind the hotel.'

'Ah!' said Gavin. 'Did you see a motor-caravan?'

'No.'

'Well, it was there.'

'Yes, but I was not on the road. I climbed the hill, but first I went through the hotel grounds and then I got over a fence, and then I went on, still up, through a very small field and over a deep ditch and through a little wood, and on to another field. I saw some farm buildings in front of me, so I bore away to my left. Farmers are surly old brutes. I then came out on the moors. I didn't see anybody at all.'

'After that?'

'I came downhill to the right and got into the main road of the town. I'd lost my pocket compass, you see. Then I went to look at the outside of the cathedral.'

'You did not go in?'

'No. It wasn't open.'

'What was the time?'

'I don't remember looking at my watch.'

'The cathedral has a clock on the tower.'

'Oh, yes, of course. So I suppose I must have looked at it, but I don't remember what the time was. I suppose I wouldn't have worried, unless it was time for breakfast.'

'What did you do after that?'

'I went back to the hotel and had a swim.'

'Then in to breakfast?'

'Of course not. I had a bath first.'

'After your swim?'

'Of course. I'm not accustomed to going about all day with a swimming-bath smell all around me. It's the chlorine in the water that stinks. So I always wash the stink off.'

'Well, I'm damned!' said Gavin, for this answer, to him,

put Robert in a category of his own so far as young boys were concerned.

'It is my grandmother's wish,' explained Robert, thus translating himself once more to the fold of the ninety and nine. Gavin grunted, but his expression became somewhat happier.

'Then breakfast, I suppose?' he demanded. Robert nodded, and said that the breakfast had been pretty good.

'And then I smoked a cigarette given me by the garage boy,' he added, 'and after that I played tennis.'

'With whom?'

'By myself, of course. Better exercise.'

'Oh, lobbing the ball high and jumping over the net?'

'Yes, of course. And then I went to the cathedral again, and saw Mrs. Cassock on the tower.'

'Ah, yes, we know about that. Good show,' said Gavin cordially. Robert wriggled.

'It was Mr. Jeffries' show,' he said. 'I didn't do anything at all. I *like* climbing towers. It's my hobby.'

'Tell us all about it,' said Mrs. Bradley.

'There wasn't much. I saw her on the tower, and some people were looking up and shouting, and she was screaming out and pointing, and Mr. Jeffries came, but I knew I could get up the stairs pretty fast, as I'm used to them, so I tore up and grabbed her, and I thought we were both going over, and her field glasses made an awful bruise on my chest, but I thought I could hear Mr. Jeffries coming up, and he was, of course, and he yelled to me to hang on. It was making her come down that was the trouble. *He* did that.'

Gavin nodded, nodded also to Mr. MacKennon, and lawyer and client went out.

'Pointing and screaming out!' said Gavin. 'Rather interesting, that.'

'George Jeffries said the same thing, and don't forget that Mrs. Cassock's field-glasses made a noticeable bruise on Robert's chest.'

'I don't care tuppence about his beastly chest! Oh, you don't mean you think she saw the murder being committed?' His tone blended facetiousness with incredulity. 'Of course, she *could* have done.'

'I should not be surprised. Thanks to the police'— Mactavish smiled ironically—'we know where the murder took place. Let us now go to the top of the cathedral tower and see what there is to be seen. We also will take field-glasses. But we must have assistance. I think Miss Baird and Miss Carter are indicated. Let us call them in.' Gavin called them. The authors looked apprehensive.

'But we don't know a thing,' said Miss Carter. She was of medium height, a thin, long-nosed, thirteenth-century caricature, with humour, intolerance, weakness and pride inextricably woven into the fabric, as it were, of her face. She had reddish hair almost gone grey, an athletic body, and the short, thick fingers and obstinate thumbs of the artist.

'We know that,' said Gavin, who believed he was speaking the truth. 'What we want from you and Miss Baird is a different kind of help. Have you any objection to coming up to the top of the cathedral tower?'

'*I* have,' said Miss Baird. 'I don't care about newel staircases, and I can't look down from heights. But I know what you're after, and I can tell you who murdered Miss Pratt.'

'Oh!' said Gavin. Mrs. Bradley looked interested.

'It was Mr. Peel,' said Miss Baird. She spoke with the unemotional sincerity of absolute conviction.

'What makes you say that?' demanded Gavin. He looked extremely startled, for this opinion was his own theoretical view. Miss Baird smiled.

'I don't know,' she replied. 'I've nothing on earth to go on except what I think. And, of course, he's a typical liar. We've found that out.'

Gavin reverted to the original subject of conversation.

'It looks as though Miss Carter and Mrs. Bradley had better go up on the tower, then, and you and I will enact the murder,' he observed.

Mrs. Bradley, provided with field glasses, led the way to the cathedral, and an interested and observant Miss Baird walked with Gavin to the spot where the murder had been committed.

As this spot had been kept as secret as possible by the police, Miss Baird was naturally very curious to see it. She had already realized that it could not be far from the cathedral, but she was surprised to discover that it was also very near the hotel, being, in fact, a deep ditch between the hotel boundary and a small market garden which supplied the hotel with most of its fruit and vegetables.

The hotel side of the ditch was almost smothered in harebells, and these were trampled and bruised as greedy trippers in England will trample a bluebell wood. Some sinister-looking pieces of roof-felting and a heavy tarpaulin covered parts of the ditch, and these, Miss Baird supposed, were hiding and preserving the more horrible and useful traces of the murder.

'Now,' said Gavin, 'I hope you don't mind, Miss Baird, but we're going to enact the murder of Miss Pratt in the way Mrs. Bradley and I think it must have been done. Come over here. Now I've just been telling you about this wonderful show of harebells and have brought you along to see it. It isn't very easy to walk along here, so you go in front. (Don't be afraid of treading on the felt and the tarpaulin. You can't do any harm now.) When I ask you to stop, I want you to gather a small bunch of the hare-bells. We found the scattered flowers, so we're pretty sure of what happened.'

Miss Baird, slightly squeamish about treading on what she deemed to be Miss Pratt's blood, nevertheless carried out the inspector's commands, and, what was more to her credit, made no comment.

'Stop,' said Gavin. Miss Baird leaned forward. The slope of the bank up which the flowers were growing was rather steep, so she had not far to reach. Feeling nervous and apprehensive, her slight body braced for a shock, she began to gather harebells. Gavin then took a tennis ball from his pocket. With a great sweep of his arm, he dropped it very lightly on to the back of her head. 'That's it,' he said. 'Did I startle you?'

'No. I was expecting a harder thing. Have you found the weapon yet?'

'Inspector Mactavish did. It's a heavy stone. It could have been picked up anywhere, so there's no possible clue to ownership. Whoever did the job probably hadn't much time for careful planning, but there are no flies on him.

We can't find any fingerprints, of course. The surface was too rough to take them. Mactavish found the stone in that clump of nettles over there.'

'Wouldn't the . . . the person have got blood on his clothes?'

'Probably not. The M.O. thinks the brick was flung on to the back of Miss Pratt's head from a short distance, the way I dropped the tennis ball on you, only, of course, with considerable force behind it.'

'How truly dreadful! But, look here, suppose it had missed? Wasn't it rather a risky thing to do?'

'The point is that it didn't miss. Far from it, as Cupid said when he aimed at the miller of the Dee and hit Henry the Eighth. Let's go back now, and see what the other two have to say.'

What Mrs. Bradley and Miss Carter had to say was simple but important. From the top of the tower it had been the easiest thing possible to follow all the movements of Gavin and Miss Baird, even without the help of the field-glasses. With the naked eye only, it was true, the couple had not been recognizable except as a man and a woman, but with the aid of the glasses it was perfectly easy to make out their identity.

'Of course, it doesn't settle much,' said Gavin. 'Mrs. Cassock *could* have seen the murder committed if it took place while she was on the tower, but that is not to say that she *did* see it.'

'There's another thing, though. *If* she saw it done, that means she couldn't have been the one to do it,' said Miss Carter, 'and, although I know Catherine is usually right about people and their ways, I had rather thought, myself, that Mrs. Cassock might have been the murderer. I mean, she is very peculiar, and if you'd seen her slam down that vase she broke . . .'

'I know we have to keep her in mind,' said Gavin, 'because she is completely irresponsible and there seems to have been no motive.'

'The ciné-camera,' said Miss Baird and Mrs. Bradley in one breath. 'It surely must depend upon that,' Miss Baird added. 'Miss Pratt must have filmed something that didn't suit somebody.' She looked thoughtful. 'How does the time work out?' she added, after a pause. 'I mean, is it at all *likely* that it was done when Mrs. Cassock was on top of the tower?'

'Well, according to the medical evidence, that would fit, but, of course, the doctors won't be tied down to a definite couple of hours or so, and she doesn't seem to have been on the tower for any considerable time, so we can't get far with that.'

'And now,' said Mrs. Bradley, in deceptively jocular tones, 'what else can you two tell us?'

'Well,' said Miss Carter, and there was a slight pause whilst she and Miss Baird exchanged glances. Then Miss Baird nodded. 'Well, there was that rather queer bit,' Miss Carter continued, but apparently her courage failed her, for again she paused. Mrs. Bradley looked interested.

'What do you mean?' asked Gavin. Miss Carter, her blue eyes looking towards the mountains, stated naively that she had forgotten what she had been going to say. Mrs. Bradley cackled.

'I think,' she said, 'that you are about to tell us of the incident at the hotel.'

'Oh, you know all about it already?' said Miss Carter, who was ingenuous enough, at this, to look disappointed.

'We should like to have your account of it, all the same,' said Mrs. Bradley, who was disingenuous enough to have made a shot in the dark without confessing so.

'Well, I suppose it wasn't particularly important, but it seemed slightly odd at the time,' Miss Carter continued. 'It was a row between Mr. and Mrs. Parks at Aberdeen. I don't know who else could have told you about it unless, in some way, Mr. Jeffries knew, because we haven't told a soul, and we thought it had all blown over.'

'It was at Aberdeen that you complained about your bedroom,' said Mrs. Bradley, 'and about the trouble that went on next door.'

'Oh, do you know that, too? Well, actually, I didn't particularly mind. It was Catherine who didn't much like it. They gave us a converted sitting-room, you see; a lovely big place, but with only folding doors between us and the next room, and there was nothing but a table in front of the folding doors and, with any heavy lorry or docks truck or anything rattling by, the doors kept jarring themselves apart. It really was a bit embarrassing, because on the first night there was a young couple next door who weren't even members of our party, and they were—well, drunk, to put it mildly.'

'The Parks had this same room on the second night of our stay,' put in Miss Baird. 'It was because we complained to Mr. Jeffries that the other people were turned out, I believe. They fought each other . . . at least, that was what it sounded like . . . and we didn't like it at all. The Parks didn't fight, but they did argue, and although we didn't listen . . . at least, not much . . . we couldn't help realizing that the row was something to do with the sea trip.''

'Then, in the morning, we found a note pushed under the folding doors,' said Miss Carter. 'I've still got it.' She took a number of papers out of a very full handbag and sorted them out. 'Here it is.' She handed a large white envelope to Gavin. There was a short and cryptic letter inside it.

'No go,' it stated. 'Nothing fixed. Devil's Elbow very fishy spot. Advise hold off. Don't want to crash, and police traps definitely functioning on the other side. Don't reply to this.'

'Of course,' explained Miss Baird, 'we knew it couldn't be meant for us, but we didn't know who it *was* meant for.'

'And you didn't attempt to return it to Mr. Parks?' Mrs. Bradley inquired.

'I intended to, but we went out early for a stroll round the docks, and I forgot it. I had stuck it in my handbag, intending to hand it back, but it quite slipped my mind until after we got to Ullswater. Then we heard about the murder and I didn't bother any more. At least'—she glanced at her friend—'I'll be honest. We talked things over and decided that to have read the letter might be dangerous for us. I can't think how you came to know anything about it, though.'

'I didn't,' Mrs. Bradley meekly explained. 'But I'm very glad to know about it now. It throws open a considerable field for speculation.'

'It makes no sense at all to me,' said Gavin.

'Sense, no,' Mrs. Bradley agreed. 'But it is very, very interesting.'

'So is *Alice in Wonderland*,' retorted Gavin, 'and that doesn't make sense, either.'

> ' "How cheerfully he seems to grin,
>   How neatly spreads his claws,
>   And welcomes little fishes in
>   With gently-smiling jaws," '

quoted Mrs. Bradley, concluding on a hoot of laughter. 'But, to be serious, I would very much like Miss Baird and Miss Carter to tell us a little more.'

Exchanging glances of dismay, the literary ladies protested that they did not know any more.

'To take one point,' said Gavin. 'If you thought the letter dangerous—and I fully agree with you there, for it's about as fishy as the writer thinks the Devil's Elbow to be—why on earth didn't you take it straight to the police?'

'It isn't all that easy for a couple of middle-aged spinsters to go the police with rummy documents,' said Miss Carter. 'The police are apt to be soothing, and then to tap their foreheads to one another when they think you aren't looking. All policemen think that all spinsters live in hourly dread of being forcibly deprived of their lives, their money and their virtue—usually all three, and, of course, in that order.' She spoke feelingly.

Gavin, who had soothed many middle-aged maidens in his time, had nothing to say to her statement, and wisely changed the subject.

'I shall have to see Parks about this letter,' he observed.

'And the hotel porters,' said Mrs. Bradley.

'You mean we've got to try to find out who Parks thought was next door to him? It's clear he had some idea in mind, and he didn't expect his letter to be picked up by one of these ladies.'

'Exactly. And the porters will help us. They must have changed over some luggage left on the landing, and so misled Mr. Parks.'

Gavin thought this theory over carefully. It seemed to fit. He nodded.

'With a biggish coach-party, the likeliest thing in the world,' he agreed. 'Good work! But, of course, his pal would have been Peel.'

Taking Gavin and Mrs. Bradley to interview the porters, George negotiated the Devil's Elbow with skill and confidence, and Mrs. Bradley's car pulled up in Aberdeen in time for tea. Jeffries was with them, and the production of Gavin's official card preceded the prompt appearance of two elderly Scottish porters. The third, they explained, was off duty until eight o'clock that evening.

'I expect you'll do,' said Gavin. 'You remember Mr. Jeffries and his coach party? They were here . . .'

'I mind them verra weel,' said one. 'Smith got ane o' the auld leddies a porr-table convenience. He's frae East London, and doesna suffer ower muckle frae manners.'

'That's right,' said Gavin, with a grin. 'That was old Miss Pew. But we don't want to know about that. Do you remember, either of you, putting the wrong luggage outside one of the first-floor bedroom doors? The room would be one of a pair separated by folding doors, a converted sitting-room, I believe.'

'Aye, the dining-hall suite,' said the porter who had not yet spoken. 'I mind we pit oot a newly-mairrit pair wha made themselves verra pairsonal to twa leddies in the neist room.'

This all sounded very promising.

'About this luggage, though,' said Gavin. 'You had to take it away and bring the right luggage from somewhere else. Remember?'

But his hopes faded when the older porter, although he admitted changing over two suitcases which had been left at the wrong door, could not recall in the least the names on the labels.

Jeffries, however, came to the rescue with a typed list.

'Come, now,' he said. 'Have a bash. See whether you can find the name here.'

The older porter shook his head hopelessly.

'I mind weel aboot the wee bags,' he said, 'forbye I had a wee fecht—worrds only, ye ken—wi' Angus here. How wis I tae ken the leddies had been in the room the nicht already?'

'Well, look here, do try to remember. It doesn't much matter if you're wrong, because we pretty well know the people it *couldn't* have been, but if you're right it may help the police no end.'

Thus prompted, the older of the two scanned the list, and after a long pause, grudgingly admitted that he thought he had remembered the name.

'But it wasna my mistake,' he protested. 'I was carrying oot orr-ders.'

'Right. Now you,' said Gavin to the other porter. The man read and re-read the list.

'I'm no verra sure,' he said slowly.

'You both handled this baggage, though?'

'Ou aye. James pit it doon and I took it up. I told him he should hae lookit at the slate, and he wouldna hae made the mistake.'

'And the name?'

Both men chose the same name. It was Peel.

'And there wis twa bags,' they agreed. Gavin was satisfied. He tipped the porters and went to the office. Here another list was produced. The Peels and the Parks had been assigned rooms on the top floor, but Parks had been transferred to the first floor when he returned from the cruise after Miss Baird's and Miss Carter's noisy neighbours had been moved. By error, the porter had been told the wrong number of the top-floor room, and had brought down Peel's baggage and placed it outside in the corridor, between the two doorways. Parks, presumably, had seen it there and, knowing that his own room had been changed, had assumed that the Peels were to be next door.

'So now to find out what the letter was in aid of,' said Gavin. He and his companions dined at the hotel, stayed the night and returned next day to Blaneden to interview Commander Parks.

Parks was more than ready to be interviewed.

'Expected it before this,' he said. 'After all, I was the one to hire the boat on which the poor girl was found.'

'Tell us all about the arrangements for that trip,' said Gavin. He took out his notebook.

'Willingly. I'd like to get it cleared up. I still can't think how on earth the body could have been parked on the boat without my knowledge.'

'The inference is that it was put there after you and the others came off, and before the two men went aboard to take the boat back to the Thames,' said Gavin, 'so I don't think that need worry you. We'd like some details, all the same.'

'Well, we docked at just after mid-day, and walked to the hotel—it was closed—each carrying his own bag. The two men were to take over at eight to get the boat back to the Thames.'

'A fair time-lag,' said Gavin, 'and you all left the boat, I suppose, as soon as you'd docked?'

'Well, we didn't hurry, you know. We'd had a good trip, and everybody was very happy, and all that.'

'I see. Anything more you can tell me? Any small point that might help?'

'I don't know of anything more.'

'Well, we shall have to see the man who let the boat to you, and if he can't tell us anything more either, then that will have to be that. Now, Commander, what do you know about this?'

He took a copy of the letter received by Miss Baird and Miss Carter out of the flap of his pocket-book. Parks read it and his jaw tightened.

'I know nothing about it,'' he said.

'No?' Gavin took the letter back. 'All right, Mr. Parks. Now, about this trip of yours. What made you think of it in the first place? Why weren't you content to remain on the coach? After all, you'd paid for the trip, and the hire of the boat, although reasonable, I suppose, couldn't have been all that cheap.'

Commander Parks shrugged his shoulders.

'I didn't lose on the deal, I assure you,' he said. 'I hope you won't let this get about, but I got back the hire from the other passengers we took. No odds to you, I suppose? They were willing to pay.'

'Oh, I see! Tell us about the hire of the boat, Mr. Parks.'

'Well, when we were in London I met a pal of mine, the fellow who owns the boat, and I told him about the coach tour. I'd booked it up by then. He said it was a pity, as he would have been quite prepared to run us up the east coast from the Thames and land us at Leith. In fact, he said that he could do Leith, Aberdeen or Inverness, just as we fancied.

'I'd only paid a small percentage of our fares for the coach—a deposit, you know—so I put it to the wife. Naturally, I was rather keen, but I soon discovered that the wife was not at all in favour. Wanted to know whether we'd have to come back by train, and asked about food and sleeping quarters, and all that. She hates trains, and likes room to stow away clothes and the rest of her gear, so I packed up the idea, more or less, and we fixed on the coach, as we'd planned.'

'More or less? You gave up the idea only more or less? You mean that all the time you were determined to circumvent your wife and go by sea?'

'Well, it was then that I thought of this way of combining the coach and the sea trip, don't you know.'

'It was not arranged on the spur of the moment, then?'

'Well, I let young Jeffries think so, but, as a matter of

fact, I had worked it all out from the itinerary supplied by the coach people. I saw that we could go aboard the boat at Leith, sail her up to Aberdeen, rejoin the coach party the second day they were there, and so pick up the tour again. The only thing was that I had to go to Leith from Blaneden to make sure that the boat was in and to find out where she was berthed. I had a bit of a toss-up with the wife, but she agreed all right in the end.'

'And Mr. Peel went to Leith with you? This would have been on the Tuesday, wouldn't it?'

'Yes. He asked me what the wife and I were going to do in the three days at Blaneden, and said that if we could think of anything good they'd like to join us. Two married couples, you see. Not a lot of fun for us, always trailing round with the maiden ladies.'

'I see. And when you mentioned the boat trip . . .'

'Peel was on to it at once. Said he should have been yachting in the Solent if his missus hadn't talked him into the coach tour, and put it that a breath of sea air was just what the doctor ordered.

'Well, then, of course, the financial aspect crept in. There were port dues, food, fuel and various oddments, and they seemed to mount up a bit, so between us we arranged to take some more of the coach party. Peel was quite agreeable——'

'Maiden ladies or not?'

'Well, we agreed to take anybody, of course, who was willing to pay the fare. We left out some of the people when the word was passed round, but——'

'I see. And the owner of the boat had no objection to these proceedings?'

'Well, we had to tell him, of course, and he wasn't too keen, but he agreed. The boat had been brought up to Leith, and he wanted his money.'

'And who made the arrangements with the two men who were to take the boat back to the Thames?'

'He did. My pal. The owner. They'd brought her up to Leith and were to go by train to Aberdeen.'

'His name?'

'Dukes. H. J. B. Dukes.'

'Address?'

'Pond House, Little Fisheries, Herts.'

'Thank you. All right, Mr. Parks. You might send Mr. Peel in next. I think I'll take on Mr. Dukes by myself,' Gavin added to Mrs. Bradley when the Commander had gone out. 'We've had a lot of trouble with some of these small craft. Smuggling, you know . . . cigarettes, guns, gold, nylons, diamonds. And that note sounded pretty fishy. He turned very dumb about it, too. Can you carry on here and see the rest of these people? . . . Not that I think there's much more to be got, except from Peel, who's still my number one suspect. Ah, come in, Mr. Peel. Sit down, please. We want a little more help from you, I'm afraid. I do hope you don't mind.'

'Some corroborative detail,' put in Mrs. Bradley. Mr. Peel settled down, crossed his legs and closed his eyes. Mrs. Bradley picked up a solid glass paper-weight and lobbed it with complete accuracy at the pit of his stomach. Mr. Peel opened his eyes wide, fielded the paper-weight promptly with one snap of his left hand, and laid it on the arm of his easy chair.

'A psychological test, I presume,' he said, with a slight sneer. Mrs. Bradley cackled.

'Reactions are always interesting,' she remarked. 'Will you describe to us in detail the day you spent with Mr. Parks in Leith?'

Mr. Peel was almost too eager to begin. The difference in his attitude was extraordinary.

'Yes, very well, I most certainly will,' he said. 'It was on the Tuesday, you know. The day before . . . well, the day before. Jeffries, the courier, had fixed up the usual sort of trip to the Trossachs and Loch Katrine. I'd done it before, but Girlie hadn't, and she seemed keen to go. I'd have gone with her, of course, in the ordinary way, I suppose, but when Parks proposed this Leith lark, well, naturally, I was on. Always prefer a stag party. What fellow doesn't?' He laughed. No one joined in. 'Well, we hired a car in Blaneden and tooled off,' he continued. 'Didn't take long to get there. Parks drove most of the way, but I took us through the worst of the traffic.'

'Which route did you take?'

'Oh, the obvious one. Down through Stirling to Falkirk and Linlithgow. The boat wasn't really in Leith proper; it was moored nearer to Musselburgh. Do you happen to know the harbour light just this side of Fisherrow?'

'I soon shall,' Mrs. Bradley replied.

'Right. Well, we went aboard and had a look round, and then Parks wanted to look up tide tables and so on, and it didn't take two of us to do that, and, anyhow, the things bore me stiff, so I left him on board, rowed myself ashore in the cruiser's dinghy, and had the good luck to run into three fellows who carted me off to play golf. I borrowed clubs from the pro., and I must say we had a very pleasant round, and another one or two, of course, at the nineteenth hole, what! I'd met two of the chaps in London, but——'

'The names of your friends?' asked Gavin.

'Meakins and Carberry. It was quite a coincidence, running into them like that. I forget the third fellow's name. The introductions were, naturally, rather sketchy.'

'Quite. Your friends' addresses?'

'I don't know their private addresses, but their business premises are both in the City. Meakins is in Potting Street and Carberry in Old Bear Yard.'

'Oh, yes, I know. One's in fish and the other's in the jute business. Now, then, you rejoined Mr. Parks at . . .?'

'Oh, sevenish. We had these drinks at the clubhouse, you see, so I couldn't possibly say to within twenty minutes or so, but it would have been something around seven. I know we had the hell of a race to get back in time for any dinner.'

'And when did you last see Miss Pratt?'

Peel looked surprised, but Mrs. Bradley did not think that the question had taken him off his guard.

'I don't know that I remember,' he said. 'I suppose she was in to Wednesday lunch, but I don't remember seeing her at dinner.'

'Thank you, Mr. Peel,' said Mrs. Bradley. Peel again looked surprised, but he rose at once and went out.

'We shall have to check this golfing story,' said Gavin, 'but I don't suppose there's much wrong with it. He knows we'd have found out about it sooner or later, so he's come across with it at once. There's only one interesting point—

and probably that doesn't matter very much. When we had Peel in before he told us he'd had a thoroughly messy, boring time in Leith, and wished he'd gone to the Trossachs. This time it's the Trossachs that he'd visited before, and the Leith trip that was right up his street. Any significance to be attached to the discrepancy, do you think?'

'I think he is just a liar, as Miss Baird suggested. *I* suggest he knew the caravan people. Of course, he has had time, since our first interview with him, to contact these business friends of his—if that is what they were—and agree upon a story.'

'If we could prove he'd done that—got them to agree upon a story, I mean—he'd have a good deal of explaining to do. I'll tell you one check we've got on him, though. He says he borrowed a set of clubs from the pro. I wonder whether the pro. will remember him from that?'

'We can see. Obviously he anticipated the question of how he got hold of some clubs, which makes one think he has something to hide.'

'Of course, we mustn't blind ourselves to the fact that, even if he *has* got something to hide, it isn't necessarily the murder. Still, he's a fishy type, I fancy, and if he *is* cooking up a story it'll be the worse for him when I can prove it. Look here, I'll go to Musselburgh and contact the pro. There's no hurry for me to go to London and interview this boat-owner fellow. What will *you* do?'

'I'll be present while you interview Miss Macklin and her uncle, Mr. Togg. I wish to carry no preconceived ideas into our conferences, but Mr. Togg happens to be at the age when gentlemen are inclined to be a trifle peculiar, not to say frisky, in their advances towards youngish women. Miss Pratt was unnecessarily enterprising in her approaches to the male sex and may have invited unseemly behaviour from Mr. Togg, although he seems to have complained to George Jeffries about Miss Pratt's unmaidenly advances.'

'I've met old Togg, and I can't imagine him acting the old goat,' said Gavin. 'Still, you never know. Look at clergymen.'

'Miss Macklin first,' said Mrs. Bradley, declining to look at clergymen, among whom she had many virtuous friends. 'I think we shall obtain more useful information from her than from her uncle.'

Miss Macklin was short, stout and earnest. Her age proved to be twenty-nine.

'Bird watching?' she said. 'Yes, I'm keen, and I've had good luck. I've seen the mistle thrush—rather rare up here, but of course it's been a warm summer—the fieldfare, the ring ouzel (you'd expect that, in wild parts and with all this heather), the blackcap (*extremely* rare, especially up here), and the dipper, of course. One would expect *him* in a land of rushing streams. I have also spotted the crested tit, a local resident hereabouts and one which I had never seen before. Exciting! *He* goes down in my bird-book ready to have a gold line painted under his name when I get back—and when will that be, do you think? Can you give me any idea? I'm due back at work next Monday.'

'Give us another couple of days at the most, Miss Macklin,' said Gavin. 'After that you're all as free as air.'

'Except the guilty person,' said Miss Macklin. 'And if you ask *me* . . .'

'Oh, but we do,' said Gavin, quickly, with a glance at Mrs. Bradley, who nodded, and another at Inspector Mactavish, who warningly cleared his throat.

'Well, in confidence, then, I suspect Miss Cann,' said Miss Macklin.

'Miss Cann? Oh, but . . .'

'I know what you're going to say. You're going to tell me that this was a man's crime. But I happen to know two things about Miss Cann which are probably not generally known. One is that she's a gymnastics mistress and as strong as a horse, for all that she's turned fifty-three, and the second is that when she was twenty-eight she was dropped from the Old Mauve's hockey team for dangerous play. I happen to know because I'm an Old Mauve myself. She loses her temper, you know, and slams out at people. Dreadful.'

Gavin gravely agreed.

'And I suppose you think that a hockey stick might have been the weapon?' he suggested. Miss Macklin shook her head.

'Scarcely feasible,' she replied. 'Where would she have hidden it? But she plays cricket, too, you know, and one could always secrete a cricket ball in one's luggage.'

'Or a hockey ball,' said Mrs. Bradley.

'Yes.' Gavin made a note. 'And her present school? I assume that she hasn't retired from the teaching profession?'

'Her school? It *was* the North-West Loamlands College for the Daughters of Gentlemen Farmers. I don't know whether she's still there. She was there three years ago, I do know that, because she umpired a game against my own school. Personally, I don't think she's at all the type to be in charge of girls in their teens.'

'Loamlands College?' said Gavin, who was not interested in girls in their teens. 'Oh, yes, I think I've heard of it.'

'It is a famous school,' said Miss Macklin in a tone of rebuke. 'And now you will wish me to account for my movements on the day of the death.'

'If you will be so good,' answered Gavin, obviously taken aback by this handsome offer.

'I got up at five and stalked the grey wagtail along the banks of a mountain stream about two miles north of this hotel.'

'Did you go up through the pine wood?'

'No. I crossed the main road which runs to Dunblane, and took the turning towards Glen Artney.'

'Did anybody at the hotel see you go?'

'No. I met a shepherd during my stalking with whom I passed the time of day, but I doubt whether he could identify me, even if you could find him. I am not the kind of person whom people trouble to remember.'

'Was Miss Pratt at lunch on that Wednesday?'

'I was not at lunch myself, so I should not know. I spotted the grey wagtail in the fullness of time, after a long and fatiguing walk along a mountain burn. On my return finding that I was bound to be too late for breakfast, I bought rolls and a box of dates and caught the train to Crieff and again walked far. It was then that I met the shepherd. I had hopes of the siskin, but doubted whether

I was far enough north. I did not get the siskin, but was quite pleased when I achieved the twite.'

'Ah, yes,' said Gavin. 'And when did you get back?'

'In time only for a bath before dinner.'

'And you remained with the coach party, of course? You went by road to Aberdeen? You did not join the cruise?'

'No. Uncle Togg went, but not I.'

'How was that?'

'There is no reason except that I hoped for the caper-caillie and the ptarmigan, and, of course, the golden eagle. Uncle has an adventurous and roving disposition. He is an excellent sailor, and enjoys life in a cramped environment, which I do not. I prefer the wide open spaces. There is never too much elbow-room for me.'

'Thank you, Miss Macklin. You have been extremely. helpful,' said Gavin, quite untruthfully, staggered that anybody could be quite so much like Miss Joyce Gren-fell's portraits of exotic spinsters.

'And although I realize that I have no alibi of any sort except the shepherd,' said Miss Macklin, 'I can assure you that the taking of life—*any* life—is quite abhorrent to me.'

'I believe her,' said Gavin thoughtfully, 'although there's no particular reason why I should. And now for the old boy.'

'And you'll remember what I told you about Miss Cann,' said Miss Macklin, popping her head in again.'

'I wonder how much she dislikes Miss Cann,' said Mrs. Bradley, thoughtfully. 'There was an undercurrent of malice, I felt, in some of her observations.'

D

'Yes, quite a touch of the Old Adam,' Gavin agreed. 'We'd better see Miss Cann. Of course, perhaps Miss Macklin was one of those whom Miss Cann sloshed with the hockey stick. I confess I shouldn't care to be at the business end of one with a muscular P.T. mistress at the handle. What say you?'

'And we'd better see Miss Durdle's diary,' said Mrs. Bradley, ignoring the question but not pointedly.

'Diary? How do you know she keeps a diary?'

'Mr. Jeffries said so. It seems to be a very full diary, too. It might contain some valuable material.'

'Do you really think so? Well, anyway, when we've seen Togg I'll push off. You do Cann and the Durdle, will you? You'll make a much better job of them than I shall.'

'Very well. Oh, do come in, Mr. Togg.'

Mr. Togg was an expurgated version of Doctor Johnson. That is to say, he was clean in appearance and mild in speech, but, as Gavin said later, clap a wig on him, and plant him in a tavern, and you had the great Sam and none other. He lowered himself into a chair with a deep grunt, placed his feet apart and a pudgy hand on either knee, and announced that it was a fine day.

Gavin tackled him by the direct method.

'Look here, Mr. Togg, what can you tell us about Miss Pratt's death?'

'Nothing. I hardly knew the poor girl. Why should I?' asked Mr. Togg, breathing heavily.

'Think again, Mr. Togg. You must have heard some gossip, some tittle-tattle, something that would make a man of the world sit up after the event and say, "Ha! So that was it!" No?'

But Mr. Togg was not having any of that.

'I know nothing at all about it, and if I did I don't think I'd tell the police. Too many women in the world. That's my idea. One more or less makes no difference.'

He wheezed out this opinion with great deliberation and then gazed steadfastly at Gavin to see how he was going to take it. Gavin smiled. Inspector Mactavish nodded.

'However much I might privately agree with you, Mr. Togg,' said Gavin, 'I've got my job to do, and my job at present is to find out, if I can, what enemies this woman had, and what the cause of the enmity was.'

'I can tell you one thing, and one thing only,' said Mr. Togg. He took in a deep breath, changed from Dr. Johnson into a bull-frog, expelled the breath noisily and, by this means, became Dr. Johnson again, and then killed Gavin's sudden hopes by concluding, '*I* didn't do it, that's that.'

'Well, now, don't be offended, Mr. Togg, but you did once complain to Jeffries about Miss Pratt's social conduct. Will you tell me exactly how you spent that Wednesday?'

'No idea.'

'Let me help you. It was the day on which you went by boat to Aberdeen. You remember, surely, joining Mr. Parks on his cruise?'

'Oh, ah, yes! I remember now. One thing first though. I've told you I didn't do it, but do you suspect me? Am I on your list? If so, I'm going to choose my words, you know.'

'It's like this, Mr. Togg. My enquiry so far has given me a pretty sound notion that somebody among the coach party either is the murderer or else connived at the murder. Therefore, until we can get a bit further and weed a few people out, we must admit that all thirty-two of you are suspects. Inspector Mactavish will tell you just the same thing.'

'Thirty-two? But without Miss Pratt . . .'

'I was counting your driver.'

'Bert? Bert wouldn't hurt a fly.' Mr. Togg paused and appeared to ponder. 'I'm not so sure about young Jeffries, though,' he concluded.

'Ah!' said Mrs. Bradley, leaping, as it were, into the arena. 'What of young Jeffries, Mr. Togg?'

She had been wondering which of the party would first make mention of Em's Dan Chaucer, and how soon, and in what particular connection with the murder.

'Well,' said Mr. Togg, swelling up again, 'if you'd heard him give a dressing down to Mr. Peel the way *I* heard him, you'd think as I think. And that redundant young woman was always after him. Serve her right if he *did* give her what she asked for. That's what *I* say.'

'And you really think he might have given her what she asked for?' Mrs. Bradley mildly inquired. 'I should have thought that virtue forbade it.'

'Oh, I don't wish the lad any harm,' said Mr. Togg, ponderous and just, and ignoring the innuendo which, as a matter of fact, he did not perceive. 'Not the least harm. Naturally not. He's a good young chap, and a helpful, conscientious fellow, too. Oh, I don't wish him any harm, only, as I say, she asked for it where he was concerned, and I *did* overhear him dress down Peel. Took the shirt off him properly. Mind you, Jeffries didn't know I was there.'

'You mean that Mr. Jeffries could not control his temper when he was angry?'

'I don't know about *couldn't*. I do know he *didn't*. *And* he threatened him.'

'Really?'

'Oh, yes. Told him to take his something face out of the something light or he'd change the shape of it for him. That sort of language. Ah, and for two pins he'd have done it. You can be sure of that. And the manager of that place at Arrowbridge. Told *him* off properly, too.'

'There's surely a good deal of difference, though, Mr. Togg, in threatening a man face to face (quite literally at that), and in killing a small, defenceless woman by smashing the back of her head?'

'I've nothing against the lad,' repeated Mr. Togg, 'and I don't like Peel. He's a conceited ape, and he's a slicker if ever I saw one, and he's got no guts and no manners, and I happen to know he's got a fishy reputation in the City. Used to be in on the Black Market. But this is all in confidence, I hope?'

'That all depends. But now, Mr. Togg, to *your* affairs. I was asking you, a short while back . . .'

'Oh, yes. How I spent the day. I shall have to work it backwards. That suit you? My memory isn't what it was. Getting on in years, you know.'

'Tackle it how you like, so long as we get a clear picture, Mr. Togg.'

'Only upside-down, eh? Yes, and talking of pictures upside-down, what happened to Miss Pratt's ciné-camera? I notice t'other young woman hasn't got it.'

'We haven't got it, either,' confessed Gavin. 'It makes

quite a little mystery on its own. We should be very glad to know what has happened to that ciné-camera.'

'It wasn't a bad one. I'd have made them an offer for it,' said Mr. Togg, in a tone of regret. 'Do you think somebody pinched it? Lots of people rather keen on it, you know, and she didn't have it with her. That I do know. So, if it's gone, it's disappeared from the poor girl's room.'

Gavin pricked up his ears and sat up straight in his chair. Even Mactavish looked interested.

'How do you know?' asked Mrs. Bradley.

'Saw her go out. I remember everything now. Niece got up at some ungodly hour and didn't get back till dinner. No consideration, that girl, once she gets birds under her bonnet. So I had to amuse myself as best I could. I'd already seen the Cathedral the previous day, so I collected three morning papers from the lounge . . . people had read 'em and left 'em there by the time I'd finished my breakfast . . . and went out and sat in the grounds.

'At ten o'clock the dotty woman went by, followed pretty fast by young Jeffries. At half-past Miss Pratt. She didn't see me because I was in a little summer-house by the tennis courts, but I saw her well enough. She'd got her handbag—one of those shoulder-strap things—and she was humming to herself and stepping it out pretty well as if she was off to meet somebody. I supposed it was that other Creeping Jenny, Miss Nordle, but later on I saw Miss Nordle go down to the putting green with Mrs. Amesby and Mrs. Hocking, and all the silly three of them squeaking their silly heads off whenever they missed a hole. Can't understand women! No sense of decency. You wouldn't find three men laughing and squealing in public and making such a poppy-show of themselves!

'Well, anyhow, one or two people came out and played tennis, and I watched that for a bit, and then I went into the bar for my usual mid-morning drink, and found Peel and his missus, and Parks and *his* missus, and the Wells (good sorts, those people) and old Leese, and I joined 'em at a table full of drinks, and I'm bound to say it was quite a jolly party.'

'And the time?' asked Gavin gently.

'Half-past eleven by the bar clock, and that was a quarter fast, because I checked it by my watch, and Peel agreed.'

'Thank you, Mr. Togg. It's only in your own interest that I ask the next and the last question: can you name anybody who could swear that you were never out of the hotel grounds that morning before you went into the bar?'

'Yes, the tennis players saw me. I'd come out from the summer-house then. And in the bar we made quite a sociable thing of it, and although we didn't have a lot to drink, we stayed in the bar until the gong, so I'm accounted for from a quarter-past eleven until one, in my own opinion.'

'And you are certain that this was on the Wednesday?'

'Positive. All these people I've just mentioned will swear to me, and then, if you remember—or hadn't you heard about it?—there was all that to-do . . . we heard about it at lunch . . . that crazy party on the tower. It seems young Jeffries just caught up with her in time.'

'That would seem to settle it,' said Mrs. Bradley. 'I

don't think we need keep you any longer, Mr. Togg. I think we could do with Miss Nordle again,' she added. 'Will you please send her in, Mr. Togg?'

Mr. Togg heaved himself out of his chair, tottered slightly, getting his balance and, with a deep grunt, ambled out. Miss Nordle came in, looking scared.

'I didn't do it,' she said, on a note of hysteria.

'Nobody thinks you did,' said Mrs. Bradley soothingly, 'but you'd wish to help us, wouldn't you?'

'Oh, yes, of course I would. Only, you see . . .'

'We have but one point to discuss with you,' Mrs. Bradley went on, still in the same soothing tone. Gavin, who did not know, this time, what line his partner was taking, listened with interest to hear what this point would be. 'You remember that on the Tuesday at Blaneden Mr. Jeffries was good enough and energetic enough to arrange a party outing to the Trossachs?'

'Oh, yes.'

'You went on that outing?'

'Y-yes, I did. I enjoyed it. It was very beautiful. It . . .'

'Quite so. Did Miss Pratt go with you?'

'No. No, she didn't. I even asked her to let bygones be bygones,' explained Miss Nordle, with a sanctimonious sniff, 'but she said she had other fish to fry.'

'Were those her exact words?'

'Yes, that's what she said. She said just that. "Good heavens, no! I've other fish to fry." That's what she said.'

'What did you deduce from those words?'

'I . . . well, of course, I've nothing to go on, but I got the idea that she meant to go to Edinburgh again. I thought she'd been waiting for a decent excuse, and the extra days at Blaneden had given her the chance she wanted.'

'To meet somebody, do you mean?'

'Well, that's what I thought at the time.'

'Whom do you think she'd planned to meet? Have you any idea?'

'Well, I don't know, I'm sure, unless it was the gentleman who treated us at the hotel, the day I went with her after the coach got to Scotstone.'

'The saloon bar gentleman?' asked Gavin.

'Yes. You see, I went off ladylike, as I told you, when she began to act common with the drink, so I don't know what she did after that. I only know I missed two trains at the station, waiting about for her, as I only felt it my duty, but there was no sign of her, so I thought, well, I didn't see missing my dinner because of Lilias Pratt and her goings-on, so I caught the next train, and there she was, when I got back to the hotel, in the lounge talking to the two Miss Tooleys. Not that *they* wanted her, poor things. They both looked properly browned-off and, really, you couldn't wonder! And then she yelled and screamed all during dinner, so, of course, I yelled and screamed too. I wasn't going to play second to Lilias Pratt.'

'How did Miss Pratt get back, do you suppose?'

'In a car, of course. Lilias wouldn't care who she thumbed a lift out of. She was like that, and I'm bound to say so, even if she *is* dead. Not that I wish to speak ill of her now, of course, but there it is, and the leopard doesn't change his spots, not if it was ever so. And Lilias Pratt swanking that Mr. Jeffries had sent her a note, when I knew all the time it was one of Bert Edwards' silly jokes, because Mr. Jeffries would never make a date with her, any more than he would with that funny old Miss Durdle, much though she might make her silly old cows' eyes at him all the time.'

'Thank you, Miss Nordle,' said Gavin. 'Please ask the two Miss Tooleys to come in.'

Miss Ivy Tooley and Miss Sheila Tooley were quietly helpful. They remembered the conversation with Miss Pratt, added that neither of them could stand her, and confirmed that she had returned from Edinburgh by car . . . or so she had told them. There was no reason to disbelieve this, Gavin decided, if Miss Nordle's story of having waited for her at the station was true, and he felt that it was.

'Please send in Miss Cann,' said Mrs. Bradley. Mactavish took out his official notebook.

Miss Cann was inclined to be difficult. She was a rangy, long-legged woman with a sheep's face, sleepy eyes, a voice with a down-dropping cadence, and large, cricketer's hands. She wore ancient tweeds with a woollen jumper, and her preoccupation was essentially with her own troubles.

'I've had enough bother sitting next to that lunatic, without being embroiled in a sex-crime,' she announced. She spread her large hands on the table.

'Your inference, although excusable, is not yet translated to the hierarchy of fact,' said Mrs. Bradley mildly. 'So far, we know nothing of a sex-crime. However, if you can help us to prove your contention we shall be grateful. It would certainly make matters easier, for it would limit the number of suspects so far as the coach-party is concerned.'

'Hm!' said Miss Cann. 'And what am I letting myself in for? And when do we get away from here? Term begins in eight days.'

'So soon? We are sorry to delay you.'

'I am the Organizer of Physical Training for my district. I have conferences to attend, and three Primary Schools to visit, next week and the week after.'

'Detective Inspector Mactavish will conclude his enquiry to-morrow or the following day.'

'Look here,' said Mrs. Cann, completely altering her attitude and lowering her voice to a confidential and evocative tone, 'who *did* do it? . . . In confidence, mind! And before you tell me that, why isn't Inspector Mactavish himself doing all this questioning? I should have thought it was quite illegal for you——'

'Woman,' said Mactavish austerely, 'gin what is going on wis illegal I should no be a pairty tae it. Mind that. But ye're English, and an English tongue will fickle ye mair than mine will. There's aye method in a Scotsman's madness. Ane o' ye murdered the lassie.'

'Really? I should have thought by now . . .'

'I know. But we have to be very careful,' said Gavin. 'So many people have such a great deal to hide. I think we may be getting the truth, but we are not getting the whole truth, and we are very far from getting nothing but the truth. You understand me, I am sure.'

'Oh, yes, I have experience of the adolescent mind, and most of these people are adolescent mentally. But tell me . . .'

Gavin glanced at Mrs. Bradley, so Mrs. Bradley told her as much as she thought she ought to know. She told her that Miss Pratt was believed to have been mixed up in some affair in Edinburgh, although the precise nature of the affair she left to the imagination of her hearer. She did not mention dates or times, and she did not mention Parks or Peel.

'Ah, yes, Edinburgh,' said Miss Cann, with an assumption of deep knowledge which her hearers did not believe she possessed.

'Edinburgh,' repeated Mrs. Bradley firmly. 'Would you care to give me an account of your own visit to that city?'

'All I know is that we went to St. Giles' Cathedral,' said Miss Cann. 'All of us who were interested, I mean. I wanted to go, of course, and I did go . . . the Chapel of the Thistle, you know . . . and it all came up to expectations. Beyond that I recollect little, except the truly lifelike statue of John Knox with his broad Tudor shoes.'

'So you cannot assist us,' said Mrs. Bradley kindly. 'Never mind.'

Miss Cann shook her head.

'I regret it, but, no,' she replied. She sounded relieved, Mrs. Bradley thought.

'Right. Now what about Mrs. Cassock?' Gavin inquired. Miss Cann betrayed no surprise at the change of subject. She became eloquent, but no new fact emerged. Mrs. Bradley, who had taken up a large unopened bottle of ink and was juggling clumsily with it, suddenly lost control, and the heavy bottle went hurtling towards Gavin's head. Miss Cann flicked a raw-boned wrist, fielded the bottle neatly and returned it to the table. She put it out of Mrs. Bradley's reach.

'Are you going to ask me to account for my movements on the day of Miss Pratt's death?' she demanded.

'Not yet,' Mrs. Bradley replied. 'And that answer will apply to others besides yourself, so don't be worried.'

'Proof of one thing, at any rate,' said Gavin, when Miss Cann had left them. 'Now to coax old Miss Durdle into lending us her diary . . . no easy task, I imagine.'

Here he proved to be wrong, for Miss Durdle, a heavy-faced woman of perhaps forty-five, appeared complete with the diary, clutching it to her chest as a child might clutch a precious doll. It was a large, thick book, and she laid it down with some reverence.

'I thought this fellow would come in handy,' she said with smug composure. 'Nothing like an eye-witness' account, you know, what, what! Which page shall I turn to first?'

'Well,' said Gavin, considerably startled but dealing with the situation bravely. 'I wonder whether you'd mind leaving it with us for a bit? We shall, of course, respect your confidence with regard to any . . . with regard to . . . well, Miss Durdle, you know the sort of thing I mean.'

'Oh, but there's *nothing* in my diary that a *child* couldn't read!' Miss Durdle protested shrilly. 'I thought I might save *time* for you, that's all. And . . . *will* my diary be mentioned at the trial?'

'I expect it is sure to get into the papers,' said Gavin diplomatically. Courteously, but with great determination, he ejected her from the room, and left Mrs. Bradley with the diary. 'I shall get back as soon as I can,' he said. 'I wish you luck with this tome. It looks a bit of a headache to me.'

'Mr. Jeffries indicated that the diary was a full one,'
Mrs. Bradley remarked. 'Well, as the country people say,
I shall expect you when I see you.' She settled down to the
diary immediately he had gone, and read every word of
it, a conscientious but, she was inclined to think, an unre-
warding task. However, she had her notebook handy so
that she could transcribe any entries which seemed to her
of use.

The diary contained a carefully preserved copy of the
folder supplied by the motor-coach company, and the
diary itself began with a detailed list of the contents of
Miss Durdle's suitcase, handbag and hand-luggage. The
diary had formidably large pages, but every one was completely filled, as though the writer could not bear to leave
a single line, or even the spaces beneath the bottom line
and at the top of the page, unused.

All the halts on the various journeys were noted, the
price paid for the morning coffee and biscuits (it varied,
Mrs. Bradley was interested to note, from one and threepence to sixpence or sevenpence), the food provided at
breakfast, luncheon, tea and dinner, and every penny paid
in tips or for small purchases.

Miss Durdle's entries otherwise were an odd mixture of
guide-book lore and personal comment, as, under
Scotstone, for example:

'Noble prospect of vast hills encircles this palatial and
popular hotel, noted for best cuisine and most lavish
table in all this hospitable and beautiful countryside.
Met a dear doggie in the lane. Took such a fancy to me
I was afraid someone might think I was trying to steal
him.'

Followed a long description of the dog, which apparently was a brindled bull-terrier puppy.

Under *Blaneden* she had put:

'Surrounded by health-giving hills and a rolling expanse of purple heather and moorland, every prospect pleases the visitor. History crowds upon the heels of popular pleasure, and legend abounds, together with sport, combining the beauties of a glimpse into the warlike past with the paradise of rugged nature softened by the amenities of a first-class holiday hotel. Golf, fishing, bathing, boating, riding are all available. Long and short walks to suit every convenience. Took one of these walks myself this morning, greatly daring, for one hears dreadful things nowadays and most of them so *young*, but most fortunately I returned safely to the hotel grounds, escorted by Mr. Jeffries. On my way I noted cows grazing and a hen with six little ducklings, or they may have been goslings. I could not say. There was a very pretty wood, but I did not venture, as trees make me feel very nervous, especially pine-trees, which have a habit of *whispering* and then of being *perfectly still*. It is as though there were people talking in the wood, and then breaking off to *look* at one. But it was a pretty walk without that, and a nice little brook and a very nice view. Mr. Jeffries startled me at first, because all I saw was *trousers*, but when it turned out to be him it became quite my little adventure, walking alone in bonny Scotland with a personable, tall young man.'

Mrs. Bradley put down the diary and looked up her copy of Jeffries' letters to Em. Then she sent for Jeffries.

'I say,' said the young man, coming in, 'is it true that my mob can all go home to-morrow?'

'To-morrow or the following day, dear child. I expect they're restive.'

'Not particularly, but I want to get shut of them! By the way, I've been asked by the Company to investigate any claims for compensation, but nobody has groused yet except Miss Cann a bit. The others are feeling rather important, I think. Bert is to meet the next party and bring them along. They're sending him another courier.'

'Oh!' She studied the young man closely. 'Had you expected to accompany the next party?'

'Not expected to, no. I did have half a hope, but there's no doubt they think I exceeded my instructions in letting Parks do that sea-trip. There seems to be some idea that the murder ought not to have happened, and . . . Well, that seems to be that.'

'Good,' said Mrs. Bradley. 'And I say that on my own account rather than on yours. Mr. Jeffries, I have a question to ask you, and a task to offer you. The question first: on that early morning walk which you took on the Tuesday at Blaneden, would it have been possible to have seen the hen with the goslings, and *not* to have seen the motor-caravan?'

'I should hardly think so. I mean, they were in the same field.'

'Ah! I shall want you, Mr. Jeffries, to find that motor-caravan. Have you, I wonder, sufficient detective ability to run it to earth? What do you say? You saw it, and you saw the man. . . .'

'So did Peel,' said Jeffries, 'and he spoke to him. I did not.'

'Mr. Peel is a busy man,' said Mrs. Bradley evasively, 'but if you do not feel inclined to undertake the commission . . .'

'I'd like to do it, but . . .'

'All your expenses would be paid. How does it strike you? . . . I suppose you can drive a car?'

'Yes, of course! I say, do you really mean it?'

'I do. Go away and think it over, and send me in Miss Durdle.'

Miss Durdle was looking pleased and hopeful.

'Don't tell me,' she said eagerly, 'that you have stumbled upon something already?'

'It is this,' Mrs. Bradley replied. She showed her the entry. 'Did you see a motor-caravan as well as the hen and the goslings?'

'Oh, so they *were* goslings, were they? I wasn't sure. Why, yes, of course I saw the motor-caravan, and a very ill-favoured person in charge of it. It was because of him that I turned back. All men are noxious when roused, but *this* man was a *foreigner!*'

'How do you know?'

'There is no mistaking them.'

'See here, Miss Durdle, this may be very important. Can't you give me some idea of how you know this man was a foreigner?'

'Well, he was very nicely mannered, and bowed to me as I passed, but then, afterwards, he spat, clearing his throat first in a most un-English way. Then, he wore a berêt. Then, he wore bright yellow boots, with pointed toe-caps. Then, he had on a bow tie with an open-necked sports shirt. Then, he wore a sash around his golfing knickers—that is to say, at the waist.'

'Oh,' said Mrs. Bradley. 'Do you think you could identify him if you saw him again?'

Unconscious of any irony, Miss Durdle said that she could, and Mrs. Bradley, puzzled, amused and, on the whole, incredulous, returned to the diary and studied the remainder of the entries whilst its owner disappeared.

Miss Durdle, as was natural, had given considerable space to Mrs. Cassock's exploit on the tower.

'A very great to-do here to-day,' Miss Durdle had written. 'Oh, dear! A to-do indeed. My heart was quite in my mouth. That poor Mrs. Cassock! Fortunately I have no head for heights, and should never *dream* of climbing a cathedral tower. None but the brave deserve the fair, needless to say, and both Mr. Jeffries (*my* Mr. Jeffries, I venture to call him since yesterday morning) and that *strange* little boy were *superb*. The feminine heart goes out to feats of daring. That one cannot deny. And all the great lovers of history were personally brave. Ah me!

'But to record these events for posterity. It was obvious at breakfast that things were in an *upset*. At that (as usual) *garguntean* feast (or should one say *barmeside?*—my spelling doesn't look right for either word, and one sadly misses a dictionary unless one has had the advantages of a classical education) one could not help noticing that our party was depleted by one. Miss Nordle and Miss Pratt, thought I, have by no means *made it up*. Not both came on the expedition yesterday to the glorious and unique Trossachs and Loch Katrine. These mountain glens and that life-giving air. To be sure, 'twas chilly on the loch, but what of that? By the seasoned traveller (which I think I may call myself now) these things must be taken in the stride or not at all.

'But, dear diary, to revert to thee. I made one with others to visit the cathedral this morning, and how glad I am to report that no harm came of Mrs. Cassock's strange and dangerous escapade. I was standing behind the two Miss Tooleys and dear old Mrs. Binns when we saw the figure on the tower. We feared she would pitch over. The urge to do so when one is alone and terrified must be overwhelming. Then to the rescue leapt the incomparable Mr. Jeffries (*George*, say I, hugging the name to my heart) and, even quicker, I must admit, young Robert Binns.

'Now had it been Miss Pratt up there I could perhaps have understood it better. That young woman must have *things on her conscience*.

'However, all's well that ends well, and Mrs. Cassock seems *none the worse* for her experience.'

'Everyone seems to have rumbled Miss Pratt,' said Gavin. 'Anything important in that entry, would you say?'

'One thing only. It would seem to show that Mrs. Cassock, Jeffries, Robert, his grandmother, and the two Misses Tooley are innocent of the murder.'

She turned over the pages of the diary.

'This is interesting,' she remarked. 'Listen: Dear Diary, to thee, as to a father-confessor, I fly. What dost think? My darling handsome George Jeffries hath shown his handmaid a mark of special favour. Pleaded I poverty to my lord, thinking to remain in the hotel and wash out my stockings and vest when others would sally forth with him to view another unique beauty spot in this wild and romantic land. Ah me! The hills and the pibrochs!'

'Wonder what she thinks pibrochs are?' inquired Gavin unsympathetically. 'I think I see what you're getting at, all the same.'

Mrs. Bradley continued reading: 'But no, I was not allowed to remain behind. My lord would have me go with him. And oh, the wild lochs and high mountains! Oh, my wild heart and high hopes!'

'Lor'!' said Gavin. 'Indelicate old party! She must be twice young Jeffries' age!'

'Just about, I imagine. But——'

'Yes, I know. I don't believe it.'

'There have been less obvious motives for murder,' Mrs. Bradley replied. She recalled the helpful Miss Durdle and Gavin took his leave. Mrs. Bradley asked Miss Durdle only one more question.

'Was the foreigner the only person you saw near the motor-caravan?'

'Yes, the only person at all.'

Mrs. Bradley sent for Jeffries again and asked him whether he had noticed the registration number of the motor-caravan.

'Well,' he replied. 'I'm not particularly interested in car numbers, but I do happen to remember that this one began with YIO. I remember it because it irritated me that it wasn't YEO. I hate combinations of letters that don't make words.'

'The dialling system must annoy you seriously then. Please ask for Miss Pew.'

Miss Pew looked thinner than ever in a grey knitted

suit. She seated herself without invitation and made a grimace of displeasure.

'So sordid, all this,' she observed.

'Miss Pew,' said Mrs. Bradley, ' I believe you to be an honest citizen.'

Miss Pew looked completely taken aback. Clearly it was not the gambit which she had expected.

'I am a Churchillian, and a churchwoman,' she announced. Mrs. Bradley extended a yellow claw which Miss Pew, after the slightest pause, accepted much in the way that she would have shaken hands with a crab. 'And as for honesty, I hope the police have noted that two rugs have been stolen from the coach since we left this place.'

'Oh dear!' said Mrs. Bradley. 'Well, Miss Pew, I now have to ask you to account for all your movements on the Wednesday of Miss Pratt's death.'

'*Not* an unrelieved tragedy,' said Miss Pew. 'I am not a person to complain, but Miss Pratt is one less creature—I do not call her Woman—to give anxiety to those of us who have the interests of the race at heart. My movements I have here.' She produced a piece of notepaper headed, Abbie-fashion, with an address in Trinidad, and handed it over. 'And no further am I prepared to commit myself,' she added, clasping both hands with great firmness on her handbag, 'police or no police. I pay through the nose, like everybody else. The rate of income tax is quite ridiculous.'

Mrs. Bradley read the *dossier* carefully.

'I see that you have no alibi after ten o'clock,' she said.

'No.' Miss Pew hesitated, and then, meeting her interlocutor's black eyes, she said unwillingly and yet with a certain not unbecoming dignity, 'I was reading the Riot Act to Mignonnette.'

Mrs. Bradley guessed the reference correctly, but waited for an explanation.

'Mignonnette Adderley,' said Miss Pew.

'You quarrelled?'

'One does not quarrel with paid employees. I was telling her what does and what does *not* do in a foreign land.'

'To which foreign land were you referring, I wonder?'

'To which? To Scotland, of course. Once across a frontier, the travelled may still be at home, but that does not apply to Mignonnette Adderley and myself. The language difficulties, for example! Do you know that a quite intelligent-looking person in Scotstone gave me a completely unintelligible answer when I asked him the rate of exchange?'

'From English to Scottish money, do you mean?'

'Certainly. It is never my custom to pay in English money when I am abroad. One is always fleeced. I remember, before the war, allowing myself to be persuaded in Southern Spain that the *peseta* was then worth sixpence! Scandalous! Threepence ha'penny at the very outside!'

'You realize that I shall have to call upon Mrs. Adderley to confirm your alibi?' said Mrs. Bradley mildly.

'Of course. I will prime her beforehand. She is rather stupid, and she may have forgotten, or neglected to notice, the time. However, I will do what I can.'

'Thank you,' said Mrs. Bradley, who did not in the least suspect Miss Pew or object to her promptings and primings. From Mrs. Adderley she could obtain, she knew, any useful information which that harassed and underpaid person was likely to have in her possession.

'There's juist ane wee thing,' said Mactavish. 'What did she do when she'd done sorting Mrs. Adderley, I wonder?'

'We'll leave her to simmer before we ask that,' said Mrs. Bradley. 'I don't want to put ideas into these people's heads. They will exchange them, and then we shan't know where we are.'

'What about Miss Nordle, Mistress Amesby and Mistress Hocking after their game of miniature golf? Hae ye speired aboot that?'

'Not yet. I wouldn't be at all surprised to find that Mrs. Amesby and Mrs. Hocking were in the town having coffee and scones at the time of the murder. They are rather that type, don't you think?'

This prognostication turned out to be correct. What was more, the waitress remembered them, and could swear to the time. Miss Nordle, however, had not been with them.

'Now I had better see Miss Bernard,' said Mrs. Bradley, when both these points had been settled by Mactavish. The mouldy-haired passenger was querulous.

'I don't see what it has to do with me,' she said. 'I should have been playing tennis with Moxie, except that I'd hurt my right wrist.'

Mrs. Bradley took hold of the wrist and tested it gently. Miss Bernard agreed that it did not hurt at all.

'Therefore,' said Mrs. Bradley to Jeffries, 'I am inclined to accept her statement. It would have been perfectly easy for her to have told me that it still hurt. Of course, that stone could have been smashed on to Miss Pratt's head from the murderer's left hand—there is nothing to be proved to the contrary. Still, I shall keep Miss Bernard on the list, and Detective-Inspector Gavin can re-examine her, if he wishes, when he comes back from Musselburgh, and he can inquire about the wrist from Miss Moxon.'

Meanwhile Gavin was enjoying himself. It was not strictly necessary that in order to pursue his inquiries he should play a round with the pro., but he was a keen golfer and it seemed to him as good a way as any, and pleasanter than most, to hire clubs and, in the terms of Quince's rehearsal, so grow to a point.

It all proved particularly easy. Gavin described the suspected man and found that the pro. remembered him at once.

'Name of Peel? Ou, ay, I mind him weel. A wee skelpit creature, verra quick wi' his hands. I mind a foursome ahint us louped up the ba' and this Peel took it like a baseba' player. Verra soople, but pu'ed a' his strokes verra sair. I'm no' saying, mind ye, that he'd never seen gowf clubs before, but, man, it wad ha' been seldom, verra seldom.'

'And how long would you say he was here?'

'Noo let me think. Ou, ay, he was here by three-thairty, nae mair and nae less. He was here by three-thairty wi' Mr. Smith and Mr. Le Grand. They twa is well kent hereabouts. And there was anither. Him I didna ken. I noticed that he played juist the ane roond, and wad hae been off aboot six. Ye'll be frae the pollis, nae doot?'

'Why on earth should you think that?' asked Gavin, glancing down at his neat, well-shod feet.

The professional grinned.

'Och, it was juist a thocht I had, ye ken,' he replied with deep satisfaction, and Gavin could learn no more.

'At least,' he said, when he rejoined Mrs. Bradley at dinner, 'part of Peel's yarn is true, but all the same, I'd like Mactavish to charge him and Parks. I bet they'd talk themselves silly when they saw the inside of a police station.'

'I note that Mr. Peel's friends have at least two names each,' Mrs. Bradley remarked.

'Yes, that's what makes me suspicious. That and the cruise itself. After all, why *should* Parks have hit on this silly notion to do part of the journey by sea? Do you think it's of any use to have another go at Miss Nordle?'

'At present, no. She's afraid of something, but what that something is we shall not get out of her yet.'

'Tell me honestly. Do you think she did it?'

'No. She isn't strong or bold enough. She might scratch, but she would not batter another person to death.'

'Still, one good bash and Pratt had had it, you know. There wasn't much actual battering about it.'

'I do not lose sight of that fact. The operative word is "one". I doubt very much whether Miss Nordle could kill anybody with one blow.'

'What do you expect will happen if Jeffries finds this caravan? You *did* say you were sending him off to-morrow?'

'*When*,' said Mrs. Bradley firmly. 'I have every confidence in Mr. Jeffries' abilities. *When* Mr. Jeffries finds

the caravan we shall get some very interesting information, although I doubt whether it will give us the identity
of Miss Pratt's murderer.'

'I'm not at all sure about that. But why Jeffries? I
should have thought the police would have done the job
quicker and better than he could. I mean, for somebody
like Jeffries, isn't it like looking for the needle in the
proverbial bundle of hay?'

'It is like looking for the proverbial needle in the bundle
of hay,' said Mrs. Bradley. 'And, talking of that particular
expression, I have never been able to see why a needle
should ever have got into a bundle of hay. A pin from
some careless person's clothing, yes, most possibly; a
needle, that indispensable adjunct to life indoors,
unlikely.'

'I don't know what you're getting at,' said Gavin,
'but I think you've got something on your mind. What
is it?'

'Well,' said Mrs. Bradley, 'I don't want to put mis-
leading ideas into your head, but, somehow, I have the
suspicion . . . and it grows stronger . . . that although there
is not much doubt that Mr. Peel and Commander Parks
were up to something when Parks fixed up that cruise, I
doubt whether the something was murder.'

'You're thinking of old Togg's remark about the Black
Market. The bottom has dropped out of that, but, of
course, the cruiser might suggest some smuggling,
mightn't it? Look here, couldn't the murder and the
smuggling be connected? If they aren't, what's the point
about the ciné-camera? After all, it *has* disappeared. And
what about its having been a man's crime? We've

eliminated all the men, even Parks and Peel. Their alibi seems perfect.'

'Yes. Since the men (except Bert) are eliminated, we must continue to examine the women. First of all, there is Miss Cann. She has the bodily strength and skill and, so far, I have not asked her for her alibi.'

'We don't know anything about whether she had the opportunity, though.'

'And there is nothing to indicate that she had the slightest motive. True, child.'

Gavin laughed.

'And meanwhile?' he demanded.

'Meanwhile we will have another talk with Mr. Togg.'

'Why Togg? He can't tell us any more.'

'Mr. Togg is a nosey and observant old gentleman, as are so many elderly bachelors. I think it is more than likely that not only did he see Miss Pratt leave the hotel, but that he has a pretty shrewd idea of the identity of the person she was going to meet.'

'Good Lord! Do you really think so?'

'Well, it will do no harm to put my idea to the test.'

Mr. Togg, however, seemed curiously unwilling to talk. He denied any actual knowledge, repeated his former statements of his own movements on the morning of the murder, and added that he did not propose to get anybody into trouble by repeating gossip overheard in a bar.

Gavin pricked up his ears and pressed Togg to tell what he knew; but the grunting Doctor Johnson was staunch.

'So what?' said Gavin disgustedly, when he had failed (after a last threat to Mr. Togg that withholding evidence from the police, particularly in a case of murder, was a very serious matter) to obtain the pointer he wanted. Mrs. Bradley cackled.

'*You* think!' she said. 'I've given you the tip. Cannot you use it?'

'A nosey and observant old gentleman,' said Gavin, slowly. 'Yes, but . . . oh, I see! You think we should contact old Leese. But is he either nosey or observant, would you say?'

'He is even fatter than Mr. Togg, and a good deal older,' said Mrs. Bradley. 'Try him. And he's certainly a bachelor, and a confirmed woman-hater into the bargain.'

Mr. Leese was in complaining mood, and the chief part of his complaint was directed, as almost always, against Miss Pew. The weather had turned wet, and there was a fire in Mrs. Bradley's sitting-room.

'Ah,' said Mr. Leese, lumbering over to it and seating himself in an armchair. 'That's ruddy well better. What do you think? A lot of pot-bellied, noisy idiots on, dammit, another tour, have settled all round one of our fires in the lounge, although we were at the hotel several days before they came, and that old basket, Rabbit Guts, and that whining woman-servant of hers, have got the only two armchairs at the other one.'

'Too bad,' said Gavin. 'Never mind. You've got this one all to yourself. Look here, Mr. Leese, you can help us.'

'Don't know that I want to,' said the elderly Tweedle-dee. 'Don't fancy the b—— police. Pinched me on Boat Race night in 1897 and had the infernal cheek to ask me my name and university. As if I'd be seen dead in any perishing university! I'm a self-taught man, sir, and proud of it. I've got nothing against that young Jeffries except he's an Oxford undergraduate. Still, I'll say one thing. He's got a gift for language. He'll get on. That's one thing Oxford teaches you. How to be blastedly rude. Gave Peel a proper dressing down.' He chuckled, ruminated (apparently among his four chins), and then chuckled again. 'As for the women,' he added, 'takes a man of *my* experience to handle *them*. You, now,' he went on, turning his head towards where Mrs. Bradley was sitting. 'You're a bit desiccated, ain't you? Never dreamed of getting married, I suppose?'

'Three times,' Mrs. Bradley replied with great composure, 'and every time the dream came true.'

'Honest?' He looked at her with great interest and a dawning respect. ' 'Pon my soul, I should never have thought it. Well, now, young feller-me-lad, what is it you want me to do?'

'We want some information about Bert, the driver,' said Mrs. Bradley, before Gavin could mention Miss Pratt. Mr. Leese slapped a bursting trouser-leg with a hand like a large piece of pork, laughed on a high, neighing note, and leaned confidentially forward.

'What a lad!' he said reverently. 'What a master! When it comes to leading these women up the garden. . . . Bert! Well, well! What a lad!'

The opinion seemed to give him cause for satisfaction. He lay back, his eyes mellow with mirth. Gavin waited a minute and then said, after a quick glance at Mrs. Bradley:

'*All* the ladies, Mr. Leese?' To his great relief, Mr. Leese sobered down at once.

'The only one he had any trouble with was that poor silly creature that's gone. Three times, to my certain knowledge . . . and it might have been more . . . she fixed up to meet him, but young Bert never turned up.

' "I'm scared silly of her," he says one evening in the bar. "She keeps dating me up, and I'm a respectable married chap with a family," he says. "And I have to keep thinking up excuses to keep out of her way," he says. "Land herself in trouble one of these days. Surprised she hasn't already," he says. "Yesterday I had to take the engine down," he says, "to have an excuse not to meet her, and then she ruddy well come along and watched me do it." At Blaneden he ricked his back jumping over a wall to get out of her way. She was the only one of the lot who got young Bert down, except for that soft-looking girl she knocked about with. She was daft on Bert, too.'

'This is just what we wanted to know,' said Mrs. Bradley. 'Now, Mr. Leese, we come to the crux of the matter. Did Miss Pratt make any arrangements to meet Bert on the morning that she was murdered?'

'She tried to, or so Bert was saying. "Lucky for me I managed to dodge her again," he says, "or they might think it was me that did her in." Not that young Bert would hurt a fly, no more than that lad Jeffries, unless Jeffries got his dander up and gave a man a poke under the jaw.'

'Go on, Mr. Leese,' said Mrs. Bradley. 'There's something more about Mr. Jeffries, isn't there?'

'Not that I'm going to tell you,' said Mr. Leese. 'Though he *did* take up more than half the seat. But you'd better see Bert. He'll come clean, if he isn't a fool.'

Bert seemed willing to talk. He was an amiable young man who possessed the fluency and self-confidence of a barrow-boy combined with the long-distance driver's wary respect for the police.

'Thought you'd 'ave got on to me before now,' he observed. 'Yes, that's right. I *did* 'ave a date with her. Only, I done it for a joke and put Mr. Jeffries' name instead of me own. Never take a lady's name in vain, and I never 'aven't, excepting getting the present Mrs. Edwards to change hers from Davenport, but there it is Well, Miss Pratt was to be down pretty early . . . this was her idea . . . in the little bunch of Christmas trees . . . larches, sez you? . . . down at the bottom of the 'otel gardens beyond the tennis courts. Not 'arf, says I to meself, says I. Well, when old Bill Bailey turns up I clutches 'im as, you might say, I might a lifeline, and tiddly-pushes orf with him in his lorry. Saved again, says I. Like 'ow? . . . sez you. Went into Dunblane, we did. It ain't above fifteen mile from 'ere. Gets our grub . . . try a good-pull-up if you wants a decent skinful . . . 'aves a couple of beers at the local . . . funny kind of openin' hours they keeps around these parts . . . and then we picks up a couple of gals . . . 'ot stuff, these Scotchies; well, p'raps being a copper, you wouldn't prop'ly know . . . and walks 'em over to Sheriffmuir. Ah, that's what I said . . . Sheriffmuir. There was a battle or something fought there. Got back about four, I did. Anything to say about that? Course, I knowed it was all right about Mr. Jeffries, because 'e didn't know nothink about it.'

'Your pal was named Baillie. Where does he hang out? Do you know?' Gavin inquired.

'Sure I knows. First turning right, second left at the bottom of the 'ill down there. If you don't believe me, suck it and see. Only 'is real name's Gordon. I calls 'im Bill Bailey for short. That was 'is Army moniker.'

'And Miss Pratt thought she was to meet you at the bottom of the hotel garden?'

'Skirt proposes, Bert disposes,' said the driver, irreverently but with justice. 'And it wasn't me. I went and put young Jeffries' moniker at the bottom, I tell you.'

'I don't *think* so, do you?' said Gavin, when Bert had gone. 'I'll have to check his alibi,' he added, 'but Bert is definitely out, so far as I can see, if this Gordon supports what he says.'

'I'm jolly glad,' said Jeffries, when he heard this. 'Old Bert wouldn't hurt a fly unless it scratched the paint on his coach.'

'I dinna ken what this Edwards would do to a fly,' said the quiet Inspector Mactavish, 'but the young woman seems to have been a verra great nuisance to him. Aye, a verra great nuisance indeed.'

'Well, I suppose, just to round the thing off, we ought to see all those that we haven't seen yet,' said Gavin. 'What about wiping old Mrs. Binns officially off the record?'

'She is vouched for by the Misses Tooley,' Mrs. Bradley pointed out, 'but she might be a useful witness in other respects.'

There was only one other respect in which Mrs. Binns proved useful.

'Oh, yes,' she said. 'I remember the day quite clearly. What do you want me to tell you?'

'About Miss Pratt and Robert,' said Mrs. Bradley, baldly. The old lady returned her glance.

'I interfered sharply,' she said. 'Robert, of course, is only fifteen, and he was embarrassed, not attracted, by her advances. He mentioned them to no one, but several persons reported them to me, and I threatened her with the police if she attempted to seduce a minor.

Mrs. Bradley nodded. Old Mrs. Binns was formidable, she noted. She said:

'You knew of Robert's gallant exploit on the cathedral tower, of course, as you were there?'

'Yes. Robert is a Binns. I am proud of him, but I would not like him to know it.'

'And you can add nothing more?'

'Oh, yes,' said old Mrs. Binns, 'a good deal more if you wish. Robert and I had gone to the cathedral so that he could inspect the Norman work there. We were interested in the differences between South British and North British architecture.'

'Yes?'

'You sound incredulous.'

'Well, your statement does not quite coincide with others we have heard.'

'I am sorry to hear that.' She added no more. There was a pause.

'What do you know, Mrs. Binns, of the death of Miss Pratt?' demanded Gavin, suddenly.

'Nothing, except that it was deserved.'

'And by that you mean——?'

'That it was deserved. At times we were all put to considerable inconvenience. That is all.'

E

'That is not quite all,' said Mrs. Bradley. Old Mrs. Binns returned her glance for glance.

'Mr. Peel,' said she, 'has a nasty, shifty eye, and I hear no good reports of him as a business man.'

'And that is all?'

'That is all,' said Mrs. Binns. 'Of course Miss Pratt asked for trouble, and what we ask for we get in the end. And she might have become a very bad influence for Robert. That I felt strongly. It was quite a relief to be told that she was dead. By the way, I am in a position to be able to tell you of two other people who were at the cathedral when I was.'

'That's very helpful,' said Gavin.

'Miss Sheila Tooley and her sister.'

'Nobody else, I suppose?'

'I did not see anybody else from the coach.'

'Miss Durdle seems to have been there.'

'Then it is odd that I did not see her.'

'How did she know *you* were there?'

'We all compared notes about Mrs. Cassock's extremely curious behaviour on the tower. Anybody who happened to overhear the conversation between the two Miss Tooleys afterwards, for instance, could have known that they and I were there.'

'So that's that,' said Gavin. 'Now how about seeing Miss Baird and Miss Carter again?'

'We have not asked them how they spent that day,' Mrs. Bradley remarked. Gavin looked at her speculatively.

'And you still think that question will keep, as in various other cases, don't you?' he said. 'I still don't see the point, you know.'

'Softlee softlee catchee monkey,' said Mrs. Bradley, 'and talking of monkeys, I think it is more than time that I sent Mr. Jeffries off to catch that motor-caravan.'

'The old lady lied about one thing, though,' observed Gavin. 'She indicated that she took Robert to the cathedral that morning. He almost certainly went there by himself. What was her object, I wonder?'

'She is very proud,' said Mrs. Bradley, 'and will not admit that Robert's climbing gives her the slightest anxiety, or that the boy is happier out of her presence. Anyhow, she can be removed from our list. She is much too slight and frail to have committed this particular murder.'

BOOK THREE

The Actions of Dan and Others

PART I. THE CHASE

*

*'When noon was come, and the broiling heat of the
sun had most power, we turned into a village to certain
of the thieves' acquaintances and friends. . . .'*

The Golden Ass of *Lucius Apuleius*
(Translated by William Adlington)

---

[1]

I HAD A FAIRLY sticky letter from the coach people for
letting one of the passengers get murdered, but they've
paid my salary all right and, rather to my embarrass-
ment (since these unfortunate people of ours have been put
to the devil of a lot of inconvenience), Mr. Wells has
pulled off his usual hat-trick and Bert and I have each
received a cheque for ten quid. I don't mean it won't be
useful, and it was presented (after an amazingly good
speech), by young Cathleen Wells, which made it difficult
to refuse, so I'm in funds, although, in one sense, I don't
like it.

Now as to our next date: this, I am very sorry to say,
will have to be put off a bit, as I've collected another
holiday job, and such a good one that I really can't turn
it down. Our Mrs. B. has briefed me to find that motor-

caravan—you know, the one which was parked at the back of those woods behind the hotel at Blaneden—and I've just finished the first day's search. With what result you shall presently hear.

Having received this commission, my first move was to contact the people of that farm at the top of the hill to try to find out what they knew.

It turned out that they knew precious little. The people belonging to the caravan, a man and a woman, had asked leave to camp for one night only, but when they stayed three nights the farmer didn't worry. They were quiet, he said, and didn't light fires or leave rubbish about, and he thought perhaps something had gone wrong with their car, but with the usual Scottish courtesy, plus the Scots' curious gift of being able to mind their own business, he did not ask any questions.

His son, a kid of fourteen, was a bit more active, however, chiefly because, like most boys of that age, he's tremendously interested in cars. He even spoke to the man about the registration plates, and it seems that the full registration was YIO one hundred.

The kid had never seen that combination of letters before, so the bloke explained that they'd bought the car and caravan in Ireland, and that they had number plates supplied in Eire. Well, I don't know very much about the way the *Dáil* registers its cars, but I thought the Eire lettering hadn't yet gone to the third place. Anyhow, it made me think that if there *is* anything fishy about the caravan, the chances are that the owner changes his number plates fairly frequently, and that fact might get us somewhere. Or not, as the case may be.

What I *did* get from the kid was a very clear and detailed description of the outfit, and this was good because I really didn't take much notice of it myself when I saw it. You see, we didn't know then about the murder, and I wasn't particularly interested in the caravan as such, but now I know exactly what I'm looking for. Blessed be boys and their infernal curiosity! I'll never smack another head again!

Talking of boys, young Robert Binns asked whether he could come with me to hunt for the caravan. I was all in favour, but didn't like to say so. However, Grandmother Binns . . . the kid's parents were both killed in an air-raid, and she's his guardian . . . was quite in favour, too, and then Miss Carter decided that *she'd* like to join us, so we're three instead of me on my own.

Well, it seemed to me that I'd better get word in the town as to the direction the caravan had taken. Couldn't get a clue at first, so worked the garages, and struck oil at a little place called Sprechie on the road to Edinburgh.

The Edinburgh trail was rather unexpected, as I'd anticipated that the quarry would strike north to Perth and then work across to Dundee—that is, if there's anything in our suspicions (and those number plates are extremely suspicious). I didn't think he'd risk the Braemar road with a caravan hitched on, and yet I took it for granted he would follow our route, with modifications, as far north as Aberdeen. Can't give any reason for this hunch at all, as, of course, the Edinburgh idea was just as likely. It simply meant that he'd have been making for Leith or Musselburgh, which were also closely connected with Parks' cruiser.

Therefore we pushed off to Edinburgh and out to Leith, but the closest inquiries have failed to bring home any bacon; so, rather washed-up, we're spending the night here before going on to Dundee. It's now half-past eleven, and I think I'll turn in. To-morrow we're going to quarter the town and see whether we can't get track of our birds on one of the roads leading out. There are a good many ways out of Edinburgh, of course, and they're all pretty busy. Still, there aren't all that number of motor-caravans up here, so somebody may remember having noticed this one go by, but, of course, the scent is rather cold by now.

We've had another bit of luck, incidentally—or, rather, Robert has. We tossed up for beats, as we'd nothing on earth to go on, and I got the Glasgow road, Miss Carter the way out to Linlithgow, and Robert picked the road to Queensferry and the Forth Bridge. We'd combed the east side as well as we could on the previous afternoon, so we decided to leave that for the time being and concentrate on the roads leading west and north.

It was agreed that we should keep within the bounds of the city, meet at lunch, and, if nobody had any news, that we'd have another go in the afternoon, after we'd had a rest, and then spend all next day in the same way. If we still didn't strike oil I was prepared to push on to Aberdeen and pursue the inquiries there, because, after all, that's where the cruiser had put in.

However, at lunch, Robert, who came in a bit late, had a grand bit of news. Trust a kid to ferret out information! He'd done it intelligently, too, combining business with pleasure in a way I can't sufficiently admire. He'd studied the map in his guide book and had ridden on a tram as far as a road in the newer part of Edinburgh at the top of which was a school. The boys were still on holiday, and he'd happened upon a gang of them who were going to the baths nearby. Robert, who seems to be a good mixer, joined them, turned the conversation on to cars and motor-caravans and, having given a detailed description of the particular outfit we were after, it wasn't very long before he heard about it.

It had taken the road to Inverkeithing, which is a dozen miles or so from Edinburgh and on the way to Dundee, and the date when the boys (after a lot of argument) said they had seen it corresponded pretty well with what we knew. The only trouble was the number. Two of the kids had taken it down, and you won't be surprised to hear that it did not correspond in the slightest with our records.

Still, this didn't worry me much. The old number plates were so obviously phoney that we guessed they'd have had to change them when they took to the road for fear of exciting the curiosity of the police . . . the last thing on earth they'd have wanted to do if they were up to a bit of n.b.g.

Robert had gone swimming with the boys—he'd been able to hire trunks and a towel—and that had made him a bit late back, so immediately after lunch we took the road again, and made for Inverkeithing.

We had to cross the Forth at Hawes Pier and found, to our delight, that in Inverkeithing (quite a small place) the caravan had parked at the hotel while the people (two men; no women observed) went in for refreshment. This was at the midday of the fatal Wednesday, so, whether the caravan people are involved in anything else peculiar or not, it hardly looks as though they could have had any share in the murder.

Well, Inverkeithing isn't far, and it was too early to have tea. We got our information, by the way, not from the hotel itself, but from a couple of old men who were having a gossip at the roadside. Had tea at Kirkcaldy and then came on here. There's only the one main road, and it goes through Cupar, Leuchars and Newport. We stopped for a quarter of an hour at Leuchars so that Miss Carter could see the church. There *is* another road out of Leuchars, but it runs to an aerodrome, and we rather betted our people hadn't taken it, particularly as the ferry across the Tay has been discontinued. I believe it was ever only a passenger ferry, at that.

We took the car over at Newport and the chap on the ferry remembered the motor-caravan very well (we got Robert to ask; I'm glad I brought him), so we're still on the right track. We had time in hand before dinner, so went the round of the hotels—they're all in the guide book, with directions for finding them—and told the same tale at each. Some friend of ours with a motor-caravan had come to Dundee a week or so ago and had recommended a hotel, but we couldn't remember the name of it. Nothing doing. It doesn't seem that the caravanners put up in Dundee, and, of course, as, like the snail, they carry their house with them, there's no particular reason why they should have done.

In the end, we've taken rooms at the hotel nearest our exit from the town. Could only get one single, so Robert and I have to share.

You'll no doubt be surprised that we haven't got further than Montrose in a whole day's driving, but the trouble was Dundee. It's quite a centre! Roads go out from it in all directions. We discounted the south, as we'd just come from there, but then were faced with a choice of no fewer than six possible routes, any one of which the caravan might have decided to take.

We thought we'd try the less obvious ones first, although, of course, if our friends had nothing to do with the murder they wouldn't worry too much about being followed, and so wouldn't have tried to throw pursuers off the scent.

However, first we went north towards Forfar. We thought, by the look of the map, that our friends might have camped among the hills. Couldn't get wind of them, so took the turning to Glamis. Still nothing doing, and Miss Carter a bit peeved because the castle is open only on Fridays. She's improving my mind. Robert's mind don't need no improvement. He can match her, fact for fact, and they hold learned arguments at meal-times, chiefly on architecture and history. In the car, Robert sits in front beside me, and we career onwards in a blessed masculine silence, but at meal-times he entertains the female part of the *entourage*, and jolly well, too.

He hasn't managed to climb a single church tower yet, but has made up for this, in my opinion, by signing the hotel register in the name of Robert Doughnut, giving his address as Great Snakes, Viper-in-the-Marsh, and his nationality as Latvian.

But I was telling why we did only about thirty miles

yesterday. Of course, it was much more than that because of our trial trips back and forth. After we'd tried Forfar and Glamis, the next thing was the road to Perth. It's pretty well open all along there, and the road follows the same line of country as the railway. The only snag was that, although the road into Perth is dead easy, and the northward trek up to Blairgowrie ditto, once past Blairgowrie you're among the mountains unless you slide off eastwards through Ruthven and Kirriemuir.

Well, we argued the toss. It had to be that way, and fetch up at Montrose, or take the road round the coast through Arbroath. It came to the same thing in the end, of course, because we were pretty sure the chaps wouldn't have tried to take a motor-caravan over the Devil's Elbow unless they were crazy. Our bus was bad enough. Thank goodness Bert's back stood the strain! Funny how it got all right again, but a bit of luck for the coach-load, me included.

In the end, we decided to follow the Arbroath road as far as the railway bridge, and then, if we could pick up no news of the caravan, to turn back to Dundee and do Blairgowrie. Our object in choosing this route was so that Miss Carter could see Kirriemuir, the Thrums of Sir James Barrie's novels. One of the hotels is called Thrums, but as it's a temperance place we didn't have lunch there, as driving always gives me a most intemperate thirst, and a pint becomes an absolute necessity. Miss Carter drinks gin. She says it's a fuel and that she needs constant re-stoking. She's certainly energetic enough! After lunch she tore all round Kirriemuir, imbibing the local colour, whilst I read somebody else's paper in the lounge and had coffee, and Robert did a couple of miles out and a couple back (at Scout's pace) on the road to Glen Clova.

While they were gone I also did a bit of prospecting, and was lucky enough to hit on the garage where the caravan had filled up. Couldn't get the garage chap to remember the number plates, but the colour and general description, and the make of the car, were identical, so there was no doubt we were still on the right track. We've certainly had luck.

As soon as the others came back I suggested that we should push through Forfar to Brechin. Here Robert climbed two towers, one built in 1360, the other one of Scotland's three round towers and of very early date, probably tenth or eleventh century. It cost him sixpence. He prefers towers that are not open to the public!

Can't quite understand why, if the caravan was spotted in Kirriemuir, it wasn't seen in Forfar. I suppose we just happened to strike unlucky in Forfar when we went there first, otherwise we could have saved time. Never mind! It's all rather fun and we're seeing a lot of the country.

[3]

Inverbervie, Stonehaven, Aberdeen. Well, we've arrived. Not only that, but we're hot on the trail. I'll tell you. We had news of the caravan at Inverbervie and, what's more, we had news of the passenger and driver. They've gone back to being a man and a woman. It's becoming evident that there are two people concerned, but whether one is a man sometimes dressed as a woman, or a woman who can impersonate a man . . . well, it doesn't matter, although I fancy the former is more likely. Anyway, it's our caravan all right, and again the dates fit. Our coach got to Aberdeen on the Thursday, Parks and company disembarked on the Friday, and the caravan passed through Inverbervie, only twenty-five miles from Aberdeen, at about five on Thursday afternoon.

It's an easy road up the coast, and they could have been in Aberdeen by six. The thing now is to find out where they camped for the night. I wouldn't be at all surprised to find that it was near the part where I bathed. There's a wide stretch of land—a sort of common, I should think—behind all the concrete defences and things, and it's flattish. The thing is that if they *were* there there's a jolly good chance that someone saw them. Anyway, here's hoping.

Have sent Mrs. Bradley a short report each day of our doings, but so far have had no reply, although I rather expected one here, as she knows where we are.

[4]

The luck's too good to last. Not only did the caravan park here in Aberdeen before, but *it's still here*. We could hardly believe our eyes.

To begin at the beginning: I don't know whether I mentioned that Miss Carter is a particularly keen swimmer? Anyway, she is, and she suggested we went down to the sands this morning for a swim.

We acquainted Robert with our plans, but he didn't seem keen to join us. Says he feels the cold too much before breakfast, which, in a boy of his age, is probably perfectly true, so at just after six Miss C. and I met in the lobby of the hotel, saw nobody but the boots, who obligingly unbolted and unlocked for us, and toddled into the dawn.

Luckily the trams run very early here, and we picked one up and bucketed down to the sea. We didn't go to the proper bathing station, but kept a bit to the south of it. Had an excellent bathe, and dressed, as we'd undressed, behind two great chunks of the wartime concrete. Miss Carter was ready in an incredibly short time, and came round to my hide-out and said, 'Are you seeable, George?'

I was, having got past the trousers and half-way into the pullover.

'What goes on?' I asked. 'Do you want a hook and eye done up or something?'

'No, chump,' she replied. 'But come out circumspectly and not showing yourself more than you can help, and tell me whether you see what I see.'

I snaked forth and, sure enough, coming along the little road which leads down to the beach was our motor-caravan, all present and correct, and it drew up not a hundred and fifty yards from where we were. I'd seen it fairly close to, in that wood, and although I hadn't been able to remember it at all clearly I discovered that I shouldn't have mistaken it anywhere.

'We'd better stroll over and get acquainted,' said Miss Carter. 'Hurry up and think of some excuse.'

Well, that sort of thing is easier said than done. If *we'd* been in the caravan and had spotted *us*, we could have asked us where to go for some water to make the tea, or something of that sort. Nothing easier. But how on earth could two wet-haired objects without visible roots in the landscape, or obvious means of support, get contact? For a minute it had me worried, but, as is usual where the circumstances are of a delicate nature, the male partner left it to the resourcefulness and self-reliance (sometimes written off as the staggering crust) of the female of the species.

'All right, coward,' said Miss Carter, when I put it that she was less likely to get the breakfast egg lobbed in her ear than I was, 'I suppose I must go.' Whereupon she walked over to the caravan, and it wasn't long before there appeared the bloke I'd seen before, and he and the Carter indulged in earnest chat.

At the end of about ten minutes, she set off down the road towards the tram stop, turned back, and waved her hand. A hand waved back from the motor-caravan, but I had the gump to realize that her wave was really for me, and that it was good-bye to Dan Chaucer for a bit. In other words, we were not to be seen together by the caravanner.

So I remained under cover and watched, and after about a quarter of an hour, when my belly was beginning to flap with hunger and my hands and feet were turning numb, the caravan drove on to the grass and drew up again almost opposite where I was.

I forgot my frightful hunger and my numb extremities, and glued my eyes on the outfit for all I was worth. You see, by this time we'd had various descriptions of the occupants, but I myself had seen just the one bloke, and I was hoping to get a look at his companion. Miss Durdle

—bless her fat head and vivid imagination!—had given a description of somebody who couldn't, it seemed, have been the one I saw, unless he was disguised, and we'd had another independent statement that there were two people in the thing. Besides, Peel himself had given the impression of a man and wife in the caravan, and, of course, the person Miss Durdle said she saw in that extraordinary get-up could have been of either sex.

I watched closely, but still the only person I saw was the fellow I'd seen at Blaneden. He got out of the car and went round to the caravan, and after a bit I could smell his breakfast cooking. Kippers. My tum flapped worse than ever, but it didn't stop me thinking.

If the caravan moved off I was determined to follow it. After all, we'd had trouble enough to find it. You don't know what a fool you feel asking about sixty people, one after another, all strangers, whether they've seen a motor-caravan go through the village, and, if so, more or less when! So I began to make plans.

Still hidden behind my slab of concrete, I wrote a note to Miss Carter and spiked it on a bit of barbed wire away from the wind. I was sure that if she couldn't find me when she got back she'd have a good look round for a message. Then I withdrew seawards, still keeping the concrete between myself and the caravan, and so got on to the beach.

I walked along the beach towards the north, came round on to the green again, and approached the caravan openly. I hadn't been able to spot the number plates from my old position, but now, keeping enough distance not to look (I hoped) like the snooper I really was, I slowed down a bit, and strolled forward, hands in pockets, and took a rare good eyeful.

The number plates were AXOTL, and that looked a bit peculiar, for a start. Besides, they definitely were *not* YIO anything, and I don't see how anybody, however myopic, could ever suppose that they were. Oh, no! He'd changed them all right, so he must be up to some game.

In fact, I decided that all our suspicions about the caravan were fully justified, and I decided to have a word with the bloke. He was sitting on the steps they put down at the door, and was getting outside the kippers with a fork and a bit of bread and butter. One comfort about it, from my point of view, you can't scoff kippers in too much of a hurry. It's not like shovelling down kidneys or eggs, so I knew I had him treed for a bit.

'Good morning,' I said. 'Nice little doings you've got here. Have much trouble on the roads?'

He gave me the eye, keeping a succulent chunk of kipper poised on his bread and butter, and then said amiably:

'Yes, the whole outfit isn't bad. No, the roads aren't any trouble, once you get it fixed in your head that the caravan's wider than the car, and that you've got the extra length when you're passing anything, and, of course, that you wobble a bit.'

'What about the hills?' I asked.

'Don't touch 'em if I can help it,' he replied. Well, it all sounded as right as rain, and he shoved the bit of kipper in his mouth and masticated in a ruminating, innocent sort of way, and, except that his appearance was against him— he was *much* too natty for that time of day, and they were the wrong sort of clothes, anyway, for a holiday of that sort—I'd have begun to think that my suspicions were unfounded and that we were barking up the wrong tree except for those confounded number plates. I mean, apart from the YIO business, I simply couldn't believe that any car was ever named after a rather exotic sort of South American lizard. AXOTL was too much to swallow!

However, I risked one more question before beating a strategic retreat.

'On your own?' I remarked casually. He shook his head.

'Wife stopping off in the city to have breakfast and lunch with relations,' he replied. 'Can't stick this kind of holiday for long. Wanted to go to Bournemouth. Sorry I persuaded her now.'

Well, it still sounded all right, but here was my bird, and I wasn't going to lose him. So I wished him good-bye, strolled back to the archway under which I'd once come on to the beach, and, as soon as I knew I was hidden, I walked along behind the concrete and the disused pill-boxes and things, and got level with him again without his seeing me.

There was still no sign of Miss Carter, but I wasn't worrying about that. The bird finished his breakfast, got down and rubbed his hands in the grass, wiped them on a bit of newspaper, put back the steps and shut up the caravan, got into the car and started the engine. But then he got out to have a look at the wheels of the caravan.

Having come forward a bit, I slid back into cover and waited until he was back in the driver's seat and had slammed the door. I was now in a bit of a spot. I'd made up my mind not to lose him again, and yet it just looked as though I'd got to sit tight and let him fly away.

He drove off slowly and bumpily over the grass in the direction of the Old City. He had to go so *very* slowly, with the caravan bumping and bouncing behind him, that I had an idea. I thought that if only I could get across on to his left side without being spotted—that is to say, the side furthest from where I was—I could tag along just behind him, and he wouldn't spot me in his driving mirror.

I decided to risk it and cross behind him. I'd have kept behind the concrete if I could, but he wasn't driving parallel with the shore; he was taking a slanting line away from the sea, so I dared not let the angle get too wide or I might never catch him.

So over I went on to his blind side, and, although the going wasn't particularly easy and I was wearing brogues —not the easiest kind of shoes for a spot of cross-country running—I managed well enough while he kept on the grass.

But all good things come to an end, and he was heading all the time for a road. Well, to canter along behind a motor-caravan looks rather an odd proceeding, and I knew that we'd only got to reach a few people for my activity to come in for comment. Once that happened, it wouldn't be long before my man realized that I was in his midst once more.

Besides, once he got his contraption on to a road I should soon be done. The things can't go very fast, but they can go a darned sight faster than a man in flannel bags and heavy shoes.

I tried to think, but nothing clicked at all, and I had the annoying experience of hearing the bloke change gears as soon as he was on *terra firma*, and of seeing him begin to glide away from me.

'Now then, fathead!' said a voice. That intelligent woman Carter had been back to get the car and Robert. She had settled our bill, and had sent Robert to prowl at the edge of the common. The kid is Hawk-eye in person, of course, and he'd followed every move. So there I was, in our car, luggage and all, driving after the caravan, determined to tail it and to let Mrs. Bradley know at the earliest moment that we'd found it.

Of course I ought to have guessed Miss Carter's intentions, but the male is a bit inclined, I suspect, to doubt the female's ability to do a bit of quick thinking. However, I take off my hat to the sex in the person of Miss Carter, and all went according to plan at first. Our plan was to follow the caravan until it parked, and then to park, too, and not too close to it, either. It led us on to the Peterhead road, through Old Aberdeen and across Brig o' Don, and so far all was very good.

It's only a secondary road, that way, once you leave the city, and it pretty well sticks to the coast. But at a little spot called Menie our quarry branched off and took the Fraserburgh road through Ellon. It was here that he decided to stop. We thought it better to pass him, and went by at about twenty-five miles an hour, with Miss Carter driving and Robert and me on the floor of the car with the rugs pulled over us, trying to make a noise like a piece of luggage. Ellon is only a village, although a big one, and there was no chance of covering our tracks.

We didn't think our bird would suspect Miss Carter of
sinister intentions, even if he did recognize her as she went
by. But I still hadn't given her credit for the brains she
undoubtedly possesses. When we were well past she pulled
up.

'I'm going back to warn him that one of his caravan
wheels joggles rather dangerously,' she said. 'I shall point
out that I've followed him seventeen miles to tell him so.
If he *hasn't* noticed us it won't do any harm, and if he *has*
it ought to throw him off the scent.'

So out she got and back she toddled—at least, I
suppose so, but I didn't dare look out of the back window
in case he should see me, and I didn't want him to see
Robert, either, because, so far, he hadn't set eyes on the
kid, and wouldn't connect him with either Miss Carter
or me, and that might be useful later on.

Miss Carter soon came back.

'He says he's much obliged and must get it seen to,' she
said, 'but, as a matter of fact, I think he *knows* there's
nothing wrong. I don't think he doubts my good faith; I
believe he just thinks that I'm mistaken. I wonder why
he's stopped here? There doesn't seem any good reason,
unless . . . That's it! Someone is joining him here! I'm
going to drive on, and then Robert will have to slip out
of the car, walk back, and snoop around.'

Robert was very pleased and, as soon as we could pull
up in front of a parked lorry which would screen the
manœuvre nicely, Robert hopped out and I levered
myself up on to the seat again to rub the cramp out of my
muscles. My legs don't take to behaving like a couple of
concertinas.

Robert came back at the end of a quarter of an hour. He had bagfuls of scones and some news. Another man had joined the first. Upon hearing this, Miss Carter, with her usual presence of mind, drove on immediately and stopped at an hotel. She went in, Robert stood on the steps with his hands in his pockets, and I lay low again.

'All clear,' says Miss Carter, getting back into the car. I got up and Robert sat down beside me. 'They've gone by. I see now why the caravan came to Ellon. There's a station, and the other man came by train. I'm positive there's something fishy going on. How very enjoyable. Please feed me as I drive. I'm utterly starving. Good fun!'

But it wasn't as enjoyable as all that, Em, because a bit further along the road, well away from the village, they had pulled up, and we simply had to pass them again. Miss Carter waved as we went by. It was no good trying to disguise either our car or her presence in it. Robert and I were on the floor again, this time trying to look like a couple of innocent-minded fleas.

Miss Carter drove on at twenty-five. It was too fast for our purpose, but she didn't want to give the impression that she was loitering. I suggested that she should get fictitious engine trouble, and she said she would, a bit later on, and that in the meantime she thought she would stop the car and do a bit of eating and some slow and methodical map-reading, to give them a chance to get by, so that we could tag on once more.

She got out the map when we'd pulled up, put on her specs. and made the whole thing very leisurely, but what was our horror, just as she'd got the scene set, to see our bloke whizz past at fifty. He had a pal with him, too. They must have stopped to unhitch the caravan, had left it parked by the roadside, and were now in the deuce of a hurry.

'Number plates YIOXL,' said Miss Carter, thrusting the map at me and letting in the clutch.

'If it's Peterhead he can take the next road on the right. If it's Fraserburgh he keeps straight on,' said I.

'Is there a road from Peterhead to Fraserburgh?'

'Yes, it goes up through Crimond.'

'We'll try Peterhead, then,' said Miss Carter, 'and push on to Fraserburgh if we don't sight them any more.'

It wasn't too likely that we would. They had gone by at the devil of a rate, and although I don't think Miss Carter and I would have respected each other's necks overmuch, there was Robert. We couldn't let him in for too many risks.

Robert, however, always has his own ideas, and I have inherited sufficiently the blood of my poaching Welsh ancestors to connive at and even aid them. As soon as Miss Carter had struck a lady-like twenty-five m.p.h. again, Robert asked her to stop the car. He said he felt sick. She stopped at once, and Robert got out.

He hopped across to the other side of the road. There was a lorry in the distance. Perceiving the lad's plan I got out of the car, too.

Together we thumbed the lorry, a half-crown changed hands, Robert climbed aboard, and the lorry headed back the way we had come. I got into the car again and my eye met that of Miss Carter.

'Boys will be boys,' she said contentedly. 'We can soon come back and pick him up . . . or one of us can.'

In less than a minute we were pushing along at a business-like rate of knots, although no faster, I'm afraid, than the quarry. We got to Fraserburgh and Miss Carter went back to fetch the kid while I remained to keep an eye on our friends, who were parked just outside the Town Hall.

By this time I was pretty sure what the game was. The changed number plates and the dashing about from one east-coast port to another, and the fact that it is only three hundred and seventy miles from Leith to Amsterdam gave me a pretty good idea of what to expect. It was also clear that if Miss Pratt had done a bit of tactless recording with her ciné-camera she might have endangered her life. Suppose she had managed to get a picture of two or three men together who had good reasons for seeming to have no connection with one another, one of them might have felt tempted to do something about it, although a more sensible thing than murder would have been merely to pinch the ciné-camera and destroy the film.

'And now,' said Mrs. Bradley, returning these extracts to their official folder, 'we must tackle Bert again, because now that Mr. Jeffries has found the motor-caravan—as, of course, I knew he would—the Scottish police can get to work and find out what its denizens have been doing, and even, perhaps, why they have been doing it. What say you, Inspector Mactavish?'

'We'll need to be careful there,' said Mactavish. 'There

is nothing so far to connect those folk wi' the murder, but
we might speir about the number plates. Aye, we might
certainly do that.'

'I have been thinking about those,' said Mrs. Bradley.
Inspector Mactavish grunted. He, too, had been thinking
about them. Mrs. Bradley waited for him to speak first,
but all he said was, 'I canna come to any conclusion.'

'The likeliest thing is that they are signs to confederates,'
said Mrs. Bradley. 'YIO is a code signal, don't you think?
—and AXOTL is another.'

'It's an interesting idea, that,' said Inspector Mactavish
cautiously. 'Aye, it's an idea. You mean it would convey
information wi'oot the necessity of the parties foregather-
ing. Well, now, so it would. Aye, it's a notion. It's no' a
bad notion, either,' he concluded, betraying, by these
words, enthusiasm.

'Tell me,' said Mrs. Bradley, changing the subject
before the inspector's habitual caution flooded this small
area of primitive rashness, 'what would be your reaction,
Inspector, to the behaviour of a panic-stricken man who
had no possible criminal intention and yet has connived
at, if not assisted, a crime?'

The Inspector's unfathomable eye met hers. He permitted himself the beginnings of a very slight smile.

'I ken wha' you mean,' he said slowly. 'You mean
yon man Edwards, the driver. Well, mistress, my answer is
that I would be prepared to exercise discretion—
considerable discretion—if it helped towards a solution of
our problem.'

This answer satisfied Mrs. Bradley.

'I'd better see Bert alone,' she said. Gavin gave her a

sharp glance. Then he nodded. Mactavish was already on his feet.

'Ah, Mr. Edwards,' said Mrs. Bradley when the driver, who had brought another coach party to the hotel from Arrowbridge, came in to find her alone. 'There was just one other small point.' She indicated a chair, and Bert sat down. 'That time you strained your back. Do you remember? It was when you brought Mr. Jeffries' party here.'

'That's right,' said Bert. 'What about it?'

'It was too bad it wasn't too bad at Aberdeen, wasn't it?'

Bert swore.

'How much do you know?' he inquired.

'I *know* nothing, Mr. Edwards. I assume a great deal. Have a cigarette and think things out. I can make you a promise. If you will help the police—and I'm sure you will—there will not be serious trouble over what you did. Why not ease your mind?'

Bert took out his packet of cigarettes, began to take one out, put it back, returned the packet to his pocket, took it out again, tapped a cigarette on his thumb nail, lit up and smoked thoughtfully. Half-way through the cigarette he removed it, stubbed out the end with great care and put the cigarette behind his ear.

'O.K.,' he said. Distrust of his intellectual superiors caused him to add, 'You got to tell me something first, though. Who split on me? Not old Togg?'

'No, of course not. You've split on *him* though,' said Mrs. Bradley, grinning horribly. 'It's this way, Mr. Edwards,' she went on hastily. 'Somebody killed Miss

Pratt and probably hid her body, *wrapped in a couple of rugs*, in the luggage boot of the coach. There is lots of room in there when the passengers' baggage has been removed. Well now, there seems no possible doubt that she was killed on the Wednesday morning, but the murderer, or murderers, did not want the body to be left where the murder had actually taken place. This was probably due to a determination to confuse the police as to the time, even more than the place, of the crime.

'While you were away, therefore, at Dunblane with your friend Mr. Gordon, the body, (Miss Pratt was a small woman, noticeably so), wrapped in the rugs, was transported that very short distance from the bottom of the hotel garden to the garage.

'There was not much risk of discovery, so long as the murderer kept to the tradesmen's side of the hotel and among the trees, and apparently the murderer knew your plans for the day. To whom, by the way, had you confided them?'

Bert swore again, and said that somebody must have been there and seen him go off.

'What's more, the coach wasn't even kep' in the garage,' he said. 'It was too big. It was left on the concrete at the side. And the back wasn't locked neither, only when the luggage was in; and, of course, it wouldn't have been in, because they'd all have it up in their rooms. But, crikey! It must have taken a bit of a nerve to carry the poor gal about like that!'

'No, a clear brain, that's all, and an attitude of innocence. If the worst came to the worst, and the murderer was found in possession of the body, the only thing necessary to say was that the poor victim was very badly injured and was being brought in to the hotel. The murderer probably left the rolled-up bundle at the edge of the trees and reconnoitred with great exactness before venturing to approach the garage, but, once the motor-coach was gained, it would be the work of a moment to heave the bundle into the boot and roll it well to the back.'

'But them rugs might 'ave come unrolled; and then, another thing, I reckon I'd have been bound to see the bundle when I loaded up next day.'

'The murderer was prepared for that, I think, but, you see, there's where your back comes in. A very useful accident, one would think.'

'Look 'ere,' said Bert roughly, 'my back *was* ricked. Sprained, I called it when Mr. Jeffries asked me.'

'Well, we'll agree. It makes very little difference to the story.'

'You got to believe me! Do you think I'd have drove that poor little stiff all the way over the Devil's Elbow and on to Aberdeen if I'd a-knowed?'

'We've agreed that you did *not* know. I tell you that the point is immaterial. As it happened, not you but Mr. Jeffries saw to the loading on the Thursday morning, and thought nothing of the bundle of rugs. He simply took the suitcases from the hotel servants and put them into the boot. He is not an unduly observant young man. He had not even missed the rugs from the backs of seats in the coach. One was Mrs. Cassock's rug and the other was his own! It was Miss Pew who noticed that they had gone.'

'She *would!*' said Bert, in deep disgust.

'There would even have been plenty of room for the body *and* the luggage on that particular morning, too, because of the passengers who had taken their suitcases with them on the sea trip,' said Mrs. Bradley.

Bert, whose vocabulary was limited, swore again.

'All worked out!' he said. 'Blimey! What a brain! The chap ought to be employed workin' out our road and 'otel schedules, blowed if 'e never!'

'Yes, the opportunist mind,' Mrs. Bradley agreed. 'Intelligent, in its way, but most opportunists are criminally inclined. Did you know that, Mr. Edwards?'

Bert, who thought he perceived a personal thrust in this piece of information, did not answer.

'Well,' Mrs. Bradley went on, 'and now for *your* share in these matters. By the time you got to Aberdeen your back was better. You yourself unloaded the luggage. You discovered the body. You did not know what to do about it. You realized that the woman must have been killed at Blaneden, and that you had removed the corpse a distance little short of one hundred miles. You thought of the publicity for your wife and family. You thought of your job. You thought of the possibility of being accused of the murder. You panicked pretty badly, and I certainly don't blame you. You found yourself in a horrible situation. You were not even at your own home, where the police *might* have believed your story. Besides, it was very generally understood that you had had a good deal of trouble with this very importunate, not to say foolish, little woman, and for her to be found with her head smashed in, and the body in the back of your coach, would be damning for you, or so you thought.

'You lay and stewed over the matter all Thursday night. On the Friday afternoon the seafaring party returned. You longed to confide in someone; to ask advice; to share the shocking secret. You may have thought at first of Mr. Jeffries; but Mr. Jeffries is young, inexperienced, and belongs to the class which, in its self-confidence, is inclined to say "Stick your neck out and be damned to the consequences!" You did not see it like that. Well, then you thought of Mr. Togg . . .'

'It wasn't! I never! I ain't going to land the old buffer in a mess!' said Bert, with an animation which did him credit. 'I spoke out of turn before!'

'Quite inadvertently you *have* landed him in a mess,' Mrs. Bradley pointed out, 'but the police are inclined to make the mess a small one, provided that you are now prepared to be frank with them and give them every assistance. As I was about to remark, Mr. Togg is an unconventional, independent, staunch old gentleman, and he decided to help you. "What about the boat we've just come off?" says he. "Nobody on board her, and there won't be for an hour or two, until those two fellows turn up to take her back to the Thames. Let *them* find the poor girl," he says. "It will certainly be awkward for you if Miss Pratt was murdered at Blaneden and they find the body on your coach, but nobody could possibly think those two sailor fellows had anything to do with it. Let *them* report the finding of the body, and *we'll* just sit tight and let things rip." Wasn't *that* more or less the way it went?'

'You might a-been there,' said Bert. 'That's how it was! And thank God it's all come out. Him and me, we drove the bus down to the docks . . . him knowing where the boat was berthed . . . and got it . . . got her . . . aboard and put her in the saloon, and that's all there was to it. We done it before it got dark . . . that was 'is idea . . . and nobody said nothing to us. We drove down to the beach after that, and left the rugs in a pill-box. Unless a courtin' couple 'appened to find 'em I reckon they're still where we put 'em. It was a lonely part and nobody didn't go there very much.'

'I expect you'll have to take the police to where you hid the rugs, and I don't suppose they'll be very polite when you do, but, apart from that, Mr. Edwards, I shouldn't worry overmuch. You and Mr. Togg have hardly done your duty as citizens, but, unless you really *are* murderers, it will be hard if I cannot convince the police that you were foolish rather than evil.'

She concluded this homily with a loud cackle of laughter. Bert got up, pushed his chair away, took the cigarette butt from behind his ear, studied it for a moment, and then said awkwardly:

'Well, thanks a lot. It's a weight off me mind, I must say. And it's the truth, all right.'

'Yes,' said Mrs. Bradley, 'I'm sure it is.'

'But I can't see how you rumbled it,' said Gavin, when Bert had gone.

'It was Miss Pew's doing. She drew my attention to the fact that two coach rugs were missing. From that, it occurred to me that somehow the disappearance of the rugs and Bert's bad luck might have some sinister connection. As it happened, they do not seem to have had, but if Bert had not his friend Gordon and those two young women to vouch for him, I am not at all sure that I would believe his story. He is a married man, and there is no doubt at all that Miss Pratt had made herself a complete nuisance to him.'

'Yes. We're still looking a trifle askance at that alibi of his, though. And now for Togg, the artful old blighter. Fancy his pulling the wool over our eyes like that, with his solemn accounting for all his movements, and seeing Miss Pratt go off to her rendezvous, and so on!'

'He did not mislead us,' Mrs. Bradley pointed out. 'All he did was to omit from his story a fact that he felt need not be generally known.'

'Yes, I know, but . . .'

'But whether the body was taken to Aberdeen by coach or by caravan matters not much, you were about to observe.'

'Nothing of the sort! Of course it matters, and you know it. So far we haven't anything against the caravan people in the matter of the murder. It's up to Mactavish to sort them out on the score of peculiar number plates and so on. What I was going to say is that I'm going to keep a sharp eye on old Togg.'

'And I,' said Mrs. Bradley, 'am going to send to Fraserburgh for Miss Carter and the boy Robert.'

'Why? You don't suppose Jeffries will murder them?'

'No, I was not thinking of murder, but Mr. Jeffries is a lively young man, and if he gets up to mischief now that they've found the caravan, matters may become difficult and possibly dangerous for the other two. By the way, I've heard nothing yet about Miss Cann's employers. We began by trying the Ling Association, as that seemed a readier

F

line to take than to go to the Ministry, but we haven't yet had any answer.'

'We've got men trailing Parks and Peel and their City friends,' said Gavin. 'So far, no report of any subversive activities—in fact, one of the fellows is in fish, which seems harmless enough. We may be barking up quite the wrong tree. How about Mrs. Cassock, by the way? Did you manage to do anything for her?'

'Mrs. Cassock is attending my London clinic. Her relatives seem very anxious about her, as well they may be. I think I have given them a fright. She should never have been permitted to make a trip of this kind. She is quite irresponsible. I suppose they were glad to be rid of her for a bit.'

'Isn't she certifiable?'

'They are not at all anxious for that. So far as I understand matters, she made her will before there was any question of mental instability, and they don't want that will upset. And, of course, she has always been a voluntary patient, so that no institution can detain her against her will.'

'Is there any chance you can cure her?'

'There is sometimes a chance in cases such as hers. There's nothing much wrong with her brain. She is under some form of compulsory neurosis. If we can discover the cause and remove it she may well become perfectly normal. But I know nothing yet of her case history beyond what her relatives have told me. Her husband was killed in an air-raid, and her collapse seems to date from that occurrence. But there may be an earlier history. There usually is. I am expecting a report from the clinic at any

time now. Let's have a go at naughty but loyal Mr. Togg.
I fancy he's trailing his coat by electing to stay on here.
He is that kind of obstinate old gentleman.'

Mr. Togg was neither alarmed nor apologetic when he
learned that his sins had found him out. He bristled
righteously.

'And what else could I do, I should like to know?'
he demanded. 'To relieve that poor fellow's mind was a
public duty, with thirty-odd passengers depending on his
driving and guts. Of course, we'd done the Devil's
Elbow, but we'd still got to come down through the
Cairngorms.'

This point of view appealed immensely to Gavin, but
Inspector Mactavish was shocked.

'Ye'll need to realize ye're an accessory after the fact of
murder!' he bellowed. Mr. Togg eyed him and shrugged.

'Yes. I was an air raid warden,' he remarked. 'I had
quite a dishful of being an accessory after the fact of
murder then.'

'Not much change to be got out of *him*,' said Gavin, with
a chuckle, when the victorious Mr. Togg had departed
with banners flying. Inspector Mactavish snorted. Never
entirely convinced of the efficacy of Scotland Yard, he
mentally put a black mark against it for its obvious powers
of corrupting the natural talents of young policemen.
Gavin, after all, was a Scotsman, and was obviously being
ruined, in the opinion of Mactavish.'

'This Edwards now,' he remarked. 'I am about to
re-check his alibi. Verra specious it is, in my opinion. I
ken Robert Gordon verra weel. There's feathers in the
bonnet of his lorry!'

This dark metaphor was almost too much for Gavin's gravity.

'I've talked to him. He seems a respectable enough chap,' he said. 'In fact, I'm certain, and so is Mrs. Bradley, that he and those two young women are speaking the truth about Edwards.'

'I ken his kind. *I'll* sort him!' retorted Mactavish with a scowl. But Gordon, as the inspector reported gloomily later on, stuck steadfastly to his tale. It was again confirmed by the two young women who had gone out with the drivers to Sheriffmuir, for the inspector tracked them down again in Dunblane, where they worked, and their stories, taken separately, tallied completely. There could be no reason to doubt that Miss Pratt's body, small and light, had been bundled into the back of the motor-coach whilst Bert was absent, and, unless Bert had been pre-advised of the murder (which hardly seemed likely), there was no doubt that he was innocent of every crime except that of having lost his head.

'You'd expect him to be a bad driver, panicking like that at the sight of the corpse and getting rid of it in that damn-silly way,' said Gavin, when Mrs. Bradley advanced this point of view; but she shook her head.

'I should not call Mr. Edwards a bad driver, necessarily, any more than I should think a boxer no good in the ring because he panicked at the sight of a poisonous snake in his bathroom. People may panic when confronted by the unknown, but their reactions to the familiar remain constant,' she observed.

'Just as you say,' said Gavin; but he was not convinced. 'Well now, what about Miss Macklin? She's old Togg's niece and, furthermore, she's the one person who hasn't even the shadow of an alibi for the whole of the day in question. Don't you think we ought to see her again? It seems to me more than a bit fishy that's she's left her uncle to stay on up here instead of taking him back to London with the other passengers. Doesn't she live with him?'

'We can see her again, but I doubt very much whether we shall get any more out of her,' said Mrs. Bradley. 'And where are you going to see her? . . . Send for her to come here again, or go to see her in London?'

'Oh, London. As a matter of fact, there's nothing more for me to do here now we're certain of the driver's alibi. I want to get back and find out a good deal more about this cruiser Parks had out on hire.'

He departed, and two days later he called up Mrs. Bradley on long distance and informed her that there was nothing more to be got from Miss Macklin except 'a lot of blah about dotterels and whimbrels, and the migratory habits of the tern.'

Meanwhile Robert Binns and Miss Carter had made their way back to Blaneden with the report that they had mislaid both Mr. Jeffries and the car that had been attached to the caravan. Robert's personal adventures had been interesting. He detailed them zestfully. He had ridden in the lorry, seated beside the driver, until they reached the hotel where he had stood on the steps. He had asked to be set down there, and from there he had strolled gently towards the spot where the caravan was parked.

There was nobody about. Robert had waited for ten minutes by his wrist-watch. He had felt himself to be painstaking, efficient and patient. At the end of the ten minutes he had gone up to the caravan and tried both the doors.

To the average person there would have appeared no hope of entering the caravan except by smashing a window, but to a boy possessed of Robert's peculiar flair for gaining admission to the locked towers of churches, the caravan was as easy to open as a tin of Swiss ham.

'I just twiddled with a key or two,' he explained, 'and there I was. Only, before I began work, I knocked pretty loudly on each door in case they might have left somebody on guard inside. The caravan, a very nice one, has two doors and four windows. At the end where it hitches on to the car there are three windows, one in the front and one on either side. The only other window is at the back. All are covered by curtains; I couldn't get a look inside. On the starboard side there is nothing else . . . simply a blank sheet of metal—aluminium, you know. On the port side are the two doors, one leading into the saloon, the other into the kitchen. Well, I tried one or two of these'—he produced a curious collection of keys and some bent pieces of strong wire—'and it wasn't long before I'd found my way in. Then I began my search. First I tried the oven of the cooking stove. Nothing in there except a dirty meat tin. Then I opened the larder. Tinned soup and tinned fruit. Then I opened all the roof lockers. Just what you'd expect—clothes and tennis shoes. So I had to get down to work in real earnest and, after a good look out of each window (although I didn't expect the men back as soon as all that), I took one of the bunks to bits. There are four berths, but I didn't want to do too much damage, so I only tackled the one. Of course, if it hadn't yielded such good results I suppose I should have tried another, but it was really wizard. I always carry a pretty decent knife about with me and keep it sharp, and I just neatly slit along the outside edge of the mattress to about a foot. Well, I put my hand in, and the mattress was stuffed with stockings . . . dozens of pairs. I put them all back, of course, and then tried the bedclothes. The eiderdown was simply stuffed with them—with the stockings, I mean.

'I put everything back where I found it (except that I couldn't sew up the bedding again), and I decided to leave while the going was good. I had another look out of each window and waited while an old man went by. He had a good stare at the caravan, but he didn't see me and I guessed he was only a villager. As soon as he was out of sight I slipped out. I shut the doors, but did not try fiddling about to re-lock them, and I was only a yard or two down the road when Miss Carter turned up in the car. She said she had left Mr. Jeffries in Fraserburgh and that the men were there and had parked their car. Of course, neither of us knew then what Mr. Jeffries had been doing, but I told her about the nylons, and asked if she'd like to see them. She said she'd take my word for them, and she said that we seemed to be on to something pretty hot. Then we drove to Fraserburgh, but couldn't find Mr. Jeffries anywhere. Some men down by the harbour told us that a man had swum off to one of the boats. We guessed it was Mr. Jeffries because he is a sporting type of man, but I did think he might have waited for me to go with him. I wonder what he's been up to?'

This information was supplied by Jeffries himself.

PART II. THE CAPTURE

*

> '*The last novel, dear gossips, prompts me to relate how a worthy man, likewise a jester, reprehended without not success the greed of a very wealthy merchant; and though the burden of my story is not unlike the last, yet, perchance, it may not on that account be the less appreciated by you, because it has a happy termination.*'
>
> The Decameron of *Giovanni Boccaccio*
> Translated by *J. M. Rigg*

THERE IS A GOOD fishing harbour at Fraserburgh and, having left Miss Carter to go back and pick up Robert before the boy got into trouble, I went to the water's edge to have a look at things. As soon as I began to look round the harbour one of its denizens caught my suspicious eye. Among the fleet of fishing trawlers was a big sea-going cruiser.

'So there you are!' I thought, jumping to an unwarrantable but, as it turned out, correct conclusion. 'And now to get aboard you, hoping that nobody's in charge.' I decided to swim. I had two reasons for this. One was that I would have had to employ a boatman to take me out to the cruiser, and, if there was anybody on board, the boatman might have been surprised at the reception accorded to his passenger. The other reason was that, again, if there was anybody on board, this man would take little notice of a swimmer and I would merely pass the time of day, as it were, and swim ashore again. Having decided all this, I stripped to my underclothes and pushed off into the water.

Whatever speculation there may have been in lounging Scottish breasts upon seeing me in summer vest and trunks, setting off from the quay of a fishing harbour to climb aboard a moored boat, the fact remains that nothing at all was done about it. The lounging public (elderly men for the most part) watched me with rheumy, shrewd, sad, seafaring eyes, spat, watched, spat again, and that was all.

The cruiser was well out in the harbour, but I reached her all right. I couldn't see anybody on board her, so I swarmed up by means of the buoy and stout chain by which she was moored, and scrambled up over her stern.

I don't know whether you've ever tried this kind of adventure, but I should think it's akin to burgling a house. The skin is apt to rise upon the nape of the neck, and one tends to imagine sounds where no sounds ought to be. I made full allowance for the possible state of my nerves, but, all the same, unless my ears deceived me, there came sounds of loud snoring from the cabin. I stood like a statue and listened. No doubt about it at all!

This boat was built about fourteen or fifteen years ago. She must have been the latest thing then . . . sea-water-resisting aluminium alloy, fifty-five feet overall, nice and high out of the water, and capable of sleeping ten people probably. The cabin whence came the snoring was almost under my feet, so, having located the sounds, I went cautiously to work to find out who was producing them.

The boat consisted of a deckhouse amidships, a long saloon forward of this (which could also be used as a cabin), and a couple of cabins aft. There was no doubt that the sounds came from aft, so I explored that way. I suppose I'd expected to find a man, but actually it was a woman. She was middle-aged, stern-featured and, with a squarish mouth wide open, she was snoring to wake the dead.

I tip-toed away, glad of my bare feet because they didn't make any noise, and I had a look inside the deckhouse while I considered what I should do. My mind was soon made up. I'd got to know whether the boat was something to do with the caravan or not.

I discarded all remnants of chivalry, crept into the cabin, picked up a cushion from the opposite berth and shoved it over the snoring woman's face. Then I said, 'Come clean, sister. What's the perishing game?'

It sounded pretty hot, I thought. It went over big, too. She gave a sort of startled gargle, lunged upwards, and tried to throw me off, but I was in a strategic position and just laughed, thinking all the time, however, that if she turned out to be a good citizen and a ratepayer I was going to look pretty silly later on.

'So what?' I said. I didn't want to suffocate the woman, and wasn't sure how far I could go, but I deduced that if she could yammer (which she proceeded to do in a muffled but lively manner) she could talk if she liked, and I wanted her to.

'Come on,' I said. 'And it's got to be turkey, see? Moreover, I'm in a hurry. Where's the stuff?'

At this point I thought I'd better let her have a little more air, and I was carefully removing the cushion when there was a terrific bellow from the deck. I didn't have any time to think and, of course, I panicked. Instead of bolting the cabin door and threatening to throttle the woman if she didn't supply the information I wanted, I dived out through a door in the intervening bulkhead under the deckhouse, raced through the forward cabin, gained the saloon, opened the door into the forward cockpit, popped up on deck, and prepared to give battle.

The bloke, whoever he was, made the tactical mistake of following me. By the time I got on deck I had a plan of action. I slammed the last door, raced for the controls, and, before any of us knew where we were, I had started the engine.

Well, of course, we were moored to a buoy . . . a whacking big one, incidentally . . . and my apparently rash action—although well thought out by me—caught the party of the second part as I'd planned, because we pulled up with a jerk that threw me against the side of the deckhouse, and which had even worse effects upon him because I was expecting it and he wasn't. He was just coming up out of the forward cockpit at the time, and he hit his head a crack that made mine ache in sympathy. But my bolt was shot. I didn't know what else to do, because just then the woman came out of the after-well with a useful-looking cosh in her hand. I had half-suffocated her with a cushion, but I didn't see how I could slosh her, so, having switched off immediately I'd switched on, I dived overboard and pulled for the shore like Sankey

and Moody in person. Only—I didn't go too far. The
harbour was crowded with craft, so I swam round the
first of these, lay low, half-submerged, and waited upon
events. The situation was pretty, and I didn't want to miss
the effects.

I was pretty sure that the interest displayed in my
aquatics by persons ashore and on fishing boats would
soon give away my presence to the two on board
the cruiser, and so it proved. The bloke had come
aboard by means of a dinghy. He apparently was still
laid out, but the woman climbed in, cast off, and began
to row herself ashore. I spotted her in good time, and
swam gently round my chosen chunk of cover—a one
hundred and sixty foot Aberdeen trawler of about four
hundred tons displacement—and then again made for the
cruiser.

I climbed on board again and tied up the bloke with
some twine. Then I dashed about, strewing cushions and
rugs in all directions and opening cupboards and lockers.
Nothing! No tobacco, nylons, brandy, perfume, cameras,
field glasses, corn or timber or silks or gold.

I went into the deckhouse then and had a look at the
chart. Marked for Leith and then for Hamburg. 'Ho, ho!'
thinks I. 'Dirty work at the crossroads all right! This is
where I get action.'

After that it was like a book for boys, only it all
happened to be true. I trusted to luck the tank was full,
cast off from the mooring buoy and, filled with delicious
madness and the first fine careless rapture (so long
as it didn't end in seven years' hard!), I backed the
cruiser away and headed for the wide open spaces. I

sang, like the sailor lad in the song, as I stood at the wheel.

Oh, she was a sweet craft! Lively as a racehorse, easy to handle, wonderfully fast, and with an engine which could have given points to the most affectionate domestic pussy for sweetly purring.

I dropped down to Leith, took a bearing at the light-house on the Isle of May, and then I turned the cruiser's nose right into the cold North Sea. Only, it wasn't cold. At least, the weather wasn't, and I thoroughly enjoyed myself for about the next hour and a half.

Then, of course, it began to dawn on me to wonder what would the harvest be. I'd left Miss Carter and Robert properly in the lurch. That was the first thing, and I couldn't help wondering what old Mrs. B. would have to say to that, and about my having exceeded orders . . . hardly ever a safe or sensible thing to do.

One way and another, I found that I had plenty to think about. In fact, I began to think I'd made rather a fool of myself, and that I might have contrived to queer the pitch for all concerned. After all, I'd no proof whatever that the cruiser wasn't as innocent as the day.

However, whatever doubts I had as to the wisdom of my proceedings, I felt I'd have died sooner than crawl back to Fraserburgh with my curiosity unsatisfied. So I carried on, feeling bloodier and bloodier, until it began to get dark. I switched on all the necessary lights, and then it dawned on me that I was hungry and getting cold.

My underclothes had soon dried on me, and now I

remembered I'd tossed out some suits of clothes from some of the lockers. There was no other craft in sight, so I lashed up the steering, left the wheelhouse, and collected an assortment of duds. They weren't too good a fit, being short in the trouserings, tight across the shoulders, and decidedly voluminous in the seat. Still, I was clad. I hove to. There was only a slight sea running.

Then I sneaked a couple of tins of baked beans and about a pound of sweet biscuits from the galley, found a tin-opener, and carted one tin and half the biscuits to the forward cockpit. I propped up my captive and fed him beans with a spoon and then biscuits, for which kindly action, I regret to say, he did his very best to bite my fingers. He'd got a pretty big bump on his head, but otherwise seemed quite lively. Then I went back to the deckhouse, and did ever anything taste quite so good as baked beans and sweet biscuits shoved down together by the handful!

When I'd finished I lashed the wheel so as to keep us on course, and went into the forward cockpit for a pow-wow. The bloke did most of the talking. After some dark reflections on my birth and character, he told me that he knew what the game was, and that Peel had double-crossed him before, but that he knew some things Peel didn't know, and that if such-and-such thought, etc., etc. I was completely enthralled. Then I mentioned the cara-van. That went big, too. There's no doubt something very fishy about Peel, and that he had met the caravan people before we got to Blaneden. I thought as much at the time, only it seemed harmless enough that morning to see him and Parks just standing by the caravan chatting. But I guessed Mrs. B. suspected Peel when she gave me this commission.

When the bloke had finished talking I began to do a few sums in my head. I reckoned on an overall speed of twelve knots, and it seemed to me that I had altogether up to fifty hours' cruising to do. I'd left the Isle of May behind at six o'clock, roughly speaking, and it meant that I shouldn't get off Hamburg much before ten in the morning on the day after. Well, it seemed obvious that I'd have to crack on the pace a bit and try to reach Hamburg by dawn. Ten to one the people there who were connected with the cruiser wouldn't be expecting her so soon. There had been no sign that she was expecting to put to sea as early as she had done, and I didn't want tough eggs on the quayside waiting for me with knives and coshes, and by this time the parties of the second part would certainly have received a cable telling them all about me. The woman would have seen to that, and although she couldn't guarantee that I was going to take the cruiser across to Hamburg, it was only common sense to suggest that the people there should be warned of what I'd accomplished, and have been told to keep a look-out for me and their weather-eye skinned for the cruiser, which, of course, they'd know by sight.

It would have to be a battle of wits. The only trouble was that I thought I ought to get some sleep, and this was a sheer impossibility until I was anchored in port.

I had another and a closer look at the chart. I knew I was on course all right—I'm enough of a navigator for that—but I wanted to be quite certain of what I was up against once I was in foreign waters. Well, Hamburg didn't strike me as the easiest place to get into and out of, so to speak. It wasn't as bad as Amsterdam, where there's a bloomin' great boom across the entrance to the Zuider Zee, but it didn't look easy, all the same, and, of course, I'd never been there before. I knew the charting was all right. In other words, it wouldn't be like the north-west coast of Spain, where they alter the lights at will and leave you to take your chance. But, all the same, I didn't like the look of things. Besides, although I didn't know the first thing about the possibilities of a bloke with somebody else's papers being able to enter Western Germany, a slight knowledge of passports and visas warned me that it would be a fairly sticky proposition.

The darkness got thicker, and the first inkling I had that now was the time for all good men to come to the aid of the party was when I noticed a trawler's peculiar signals. I am not unacquainted with code signalling, and when an apparently self-engrossed trawler sent out Morse flashes which spelt, without any doubt, AXOTL, I began to sit up and take notice. I hadn't seen a flag-locker on board my craft, and, even if I had, I didn't have time to use it, so I tooted on the fog-signal 'YIO–YIO–YIO' like mad, raced to the cockpit, gagged the prisoner, and then repeated my reply. But my legs felt like jelly, none the less.

However, nothing else happened. I lost sight of her masthead lights at last, and then I suppose I went to sleep, off and on, and then it was morning. The first thing I saw was the trawler. She had AXOTL painted on a board which two men lowered over the side. I hazarded a guess as to what they were up to, and I decided to bluff things out. They had stopped their engines, so I brought my cruiser alongside. A bearded chap stuck his head out of a porthole. I'd put a tarpaulin over my prisoner.

'Who are you? Where's Makelion?' demanded the bearded chap.

'I'm YIO and AXOTL, reporting from Leith, from Aberdeen and from Fraserburgh, and from anywhere else you like,' I said. 'The point is, give me the stuff. The boss is waiting. What's more, he's getting impatient.'

Well, they gave me the stuff—a barrel of stinking fish! But the trouble was that they insisted on accompanying me on my way back to the Scottish coast and, until darkness fell, I didn't see how to get away from them without arousing their suspicions. So I kept the cruiser at a steady seven knots, and the trawler kept alongside me at a distance of twenty-five yards, and time passed.

Then the luck turned again. Just as I was wondering whether to cram on speed and see whether I could outdistance the trawler, the chaps on board her began yelling and pointing. Then I saw what they were looking at. They turned about and ordered me to do the same, but instead I crammed on speed and pelted to meet the Admiralty vessel I'd seen. You see, I'd decided to take a look at the barrel of fish they'd given me, and I'd found myself with about two million pounds worth of diamonds in the cabin! Those blokes had gutted the fish and shoved the diamonds in between the cods' roes and things. The trawler was out from Amsterdam with a cargo of illicit sparklers. And, Lord! Did that fish stink!

I soon signalled the warship.

'I've got diamonds on board,' I said to the bloke in charge of the boat they sent away. 'All above board and according to Cocker, you know. I'd like to come aboard and explain.'

'Not half you won't,' more or less retorted the officer. 'We've been told to look out for you gentlemen. You can stay where you are. We'll put a couple of men on board to bring you and your craft into port. Where did you think you were bound for?'

'Fraserburgh,' I said, not liking his tone overmuch. 'I'm connected with the police.'

'Like hell you are,' he said, quite good-natured, but giving me the eye. So they put an officer and three ratings on board with me while the sloop went after the trawler. The sloop was one of a special patrol. It was one of the 'ghost ships' in fact. They take action against contraband traders and are assisted by little fast launches which explore the creeks and estuaries and are kept in touch with by high-frequency radio-telephony on a secret wavelength which other sources can't tap.

I heard all about it from the chap who was put to guard me. (Well, I don't mean *all* about it, of course, because it's secret, but enough to give me an idea of what goes on.) It seems that they've had their eye on what he was pleased to call *my* little outfit for several weeks, and were certain they'd catch 'us' out soon. Luckily for me they were in touch with the port authorities at Tilbury, and they soon connected me with Scotland Yard.

Detective-Inspector Gavin swore to my *bona fides* from London, and everything ended well.

Only one thing I did wrong. Just think how rich I might be if I hadn't yielded up to the authorities the fruits of my brilliant *coup!* Imagine us at Monte Carlo

Em . . . you dripping with mink and me with a gold albert watch-chain!

And guess what! There's a pub in a village not far from here. It's called *The Devil's Elbow*. Of course, it's named after the Pass, not after the clue on the body, but Parks seems to have been fool enough to mention it in a note he sent to Peel.

BOOK FOUR

Recapitulation by Those Concerned

*

'It makes a good, dramatic biographer's tale of virtue and villainy, and one perfectly credible in countries where so iniquitous a custom prevails.'

Eric Blom: *Music in England*

'I walked to that delightful place Crakyhall with a delightful young man beloved by all his friends, especially by me his loveress, but I must not talk any more about him for Isa said it is not proper for to speak of gentalmen but I will never forget him!'

Marjorie Fleming: *Diary at Braehead*

'Fighting is what ladies is not qualyfied for, they would not make a good figure in battle or in a duel. Alas! we females are of little use to our country. The history of all the malcontents as ever was hanged is amusing.'

Marjorie Fleming: *Diary at Braehead*

'Well, well,' said Mrs. Bradley, who, needless to say, had enjoyed Dan's artless narrative more than did his Em when she received the lengthy scrawl. 'Mr. Jeffries has connected the caravan with some very interesting activities. He seems to be a more enterprising young man than some of us might have supposed.'

This was a crack against Gavin, who, after a first

meeting with the tall youth, had referred to him, disparagingly, as 'that long-haired, hairy-bagged type,' and had betted, in a pugnacious, wrong-headed Scottish way, that he would not have had the guts to commit the murder.

In response to Mrs. Bradley's verbal nudge upon the subject, he demanded:

'Who said the caravan *wasn't* connected with the sea?'

It was a rhetorical question, and Mrs. Bradley did not attempt to answer it. In any case, Mactavish was at her elbow with another and more pertinent query.

'Yon Parks,' he said. 'There's nae doubt contraband was run from Leith to Aberdeen in that wee boat he hired. But, mistress, what could that contraband be? It must have been something verra sma', for he had seven pairsons in the boat wi' him. It must have been something that took up verra little room and was easily hidden awa'. Ye wouldna get the leddies to sleep on mattresses stuffed with nylons! It would be like the soft-boned princess and the pea! And as for stinking fush . . .!'

'Yes, I know. What would you say to a small but valuable collection of stamps? No doubt all is grist that comes to a smuggler's mill.'

'It would fit. Aye, it would fit verra weel. The idea would be to get them for shipment to America. It's been done before. Weel, we must surprise the truth oot o' Parks ae road or anither.' He chuckled grimly.

Mrs. Bradley nodded. She added that there were still the contents of a certain letter to be investigated.

'Ou, aye, I havena forgotten that. I have given it a certain amount o' thocht. I've had a couple of men at the wee pub in Kilcrimmon, the *Devil's Elbow*, ye ken, and I think we're on tae something there. Gin there *is* a body there wha kens ocht, my lads will sort him!'

'The only thing I can't understand,' said Jeffries, 'is why the chaps in the trawler came across quite so readily with the diamonds. I mean, I realize that they recognized my boat, and probably were glad enough to get shut of dangerous stuff, but was that really enough when they didn't know me from Adam?'

'Och, that was your tootin',' admitted Mactavish. 'You'll mind . . . or maybe you will not . . . Mrs. Bradley thought the queer letters and numbers on the caravan were a code?'

'Yes, I think I did hear that.'

'Aye, weel, we experimented wi' the wee boat ye apprehended. . . .' Jeffries grinned appreciatively at this carefully chosen word . . . 'and we found that when ye sounded your hooter—ye'll mind ye sounded YIO?—ye automatically switched on the letters AXOTL from the masthead in lights. Now the meaning of the letters isna as clear as we could wish, but we are o' the opinion that they convey some sort o' warning. At any rate, there's nae doot at a' that they're a signal, as Mrs. Bradley guessed about the caravan.'

'Oh, I see. Talking of the caravan, though, aren't the laws about the things rather tough up here? I thought I'd read . . .'

'They're no as tough as they're going to be,' said Mactavish, with his usual joy in other people's troubles. 'By

the time the new Public Health Act is in, ye'll have difficulty in camping anywhere in ane o' those contraptions,
especially wi'in the purlieus o' Edinburgh!' He nodded,
pleased at the thought of holiday-makers put to inconvenience. 'Mind ye,' he added, less happily, 'I'll tell ye
this. Further north I'm no saying that they'll tak' unco'
notice, even o' a Public Health Act!'

Jeffries said he was glad to hear it.

'I'll need you to identify those caravan folks when we
catch them,' said Mactavish, 'and that will be at any time
the noo.'

The next report concerned the diamonds found by
Jeffries in the fish.

'So there we are,' said Inspector Mactavish. 'Mind ye,
we've had our suspicions, and it's a lucky thing for Mr.
Jeffries he had hold of the right end o' the stick. Forbye,
gin he hadna, I doubt whether I could ha' saved him frae
the Fiscal.'

This Caledonian threat left Mrs. Bradley unmoved.

'Fish!' she commented, with a dryness which threatened
the inspector with apoplexy. 'Diamonds in fish! Brought
in under the very noses of the harbour police! And to
think that the Roman oyster, in its decay, breeds pearls of
rare price for nothing.'

'I tell ye,' said the Inspector, speaking ferociously, 'that
oysters are ae thing, aye, and that pearls are ae thing,
too! But diamonds! Who, in heaven's name, would think
to connect diamonds wi' fish?'

Mrs. Bradley, unreasonably pleased with Jeffries and
his idiotic exploit, did not reply to this question. Instead,
she said, with apparent inconsequence:

'You know, Inspector, I think I shall buy a motor caravan. It can be either mobile or static, as circumstances demand; it is of an apparently innocuous nature but can be initiated into the mysteries of crime; it is hybrid; it fulfils all the demands of both worlds, being simple, expensive, two-, three- or four-dimensional, and, although not always a very present help in time of trouble, it indicates innocence, a belief in the tonic virtues of fresh air and the changing scene, a reliance upon pastoral pleasures. It is probably the last resort of the patient; it combines the independence of the gypsies with most of the creature comforts of the modern bungalow. Yes, I think I must have one.'

'Diogenes and his tub!' said Mactavish with unexpected felicity.

'Well, now,' said Gavin, when Mactavish had taken over the smugglers, including Parks and Peel, and the murder had been handed to Scotland Yard officially for solution, 'so far I've worked it out like this: those members of the coach party most likely to cause trouble were, in order of wickedness, Mrs. Cassock, Miss Pratt, Miss Pew, Peel, Miss Nordle, Miss Cann, and, a long way after all of them, old Leese and Parks. I don't mean I necessarily think of Mrs. Cassock as wicked, because I'm not sure how much she knows of what she does, but you think that *legally* (which, apparently, is not the same thing as *medically* when you're referring to the obviously potty) if she did anything really wrong, and got pinched for it, she'd be considered fit to plead. That is to say, according to what I can gather from your official jargon (which, if you ask me, was created only to confound), Mrs. Cassock perfectly well knows the difference between right and wrong, and could be held responsible in law for her actions.

'But, you see, apart from cigarette-tearing, and some vase and cup smashing, some long time of chain-smoking followed by complete non-smoking, some whining and complaining, and then her queer outburst at Elgin and her quite extraordinary antics on the cathedral tower she's got a clean sheet, so far as we know. The fact that she spent a few months as a voluntary patient in a mental hospital apparently doesn't necessarily place her among the legally demented!'

Mrs. Bradley nodded. She was anxious to hear all his conclusions before she advanced her own. He continued moodily:

'Well, that seems to be that, and it brings us to object number two . . . and this object is mineral . . . dynamite, in fact! . . . the murdered Miss Pratt. She asked for trouble with both hands, according to Bert, Jeffries and old Mrs. Binns, and, if their tales are true, really one can't but agree. She even tried her games on with Robert, but his grandmother seems to have kept her eyes open, and put a stop to that!

'Anyway, Mactavish and I maintain that, Miss Pratt being what she was, a menace to every thinking man, her murder was a man's crime, and so all we have to do is to line up the men of the party and have another stab at their alibis. We needn't bother about motive. It's plain enough to everybody except you, who have some dim psychiatric reason of your own for dismissing our intelligent conclusions with hoots of mirth, that the Pratt, in her girlish enthusiasm, had got some poor bloke into the soup, and he bumped her off before she could blackmail him by threatening to tell his missus.

'Simple, obvious, and yet, I think, profound. True-to-life, you see, and up almost anybody's street. But will you content yourself with this easy, rational theory? You say you're keeping an open mind about the sex of Miss Pratt's aggressor. That means, if I've learnt anything of your devious mind, that you're somehow pretty sure it was a woman. I've nothing much against it, except that women don't go about bashing other women on the head with chunks of rock.'

'I don't think the murder was planned, you know,' said Mrs. Bradley mildly.

'All right. Let's take the other people concerned. Against Miss Pew and old Leese there isn't, so far, a breath of suspicion. Miss Pew seems to have sized-up Pratt the first day and completely ignored her afterwards. They'd have nothing at all in common, anyway, and, so far as we know, they never even sat at the same table for any of their meals, or so much as exchanged two words, so I can't see what Miss Pew could have had against her, apart from the fact that I'm positive the vinegar-tongued old nuisance would consider it the most terribly bad form to commit murder, no matter what the temptation.'

'Hear, hear,' agreed his auditor, grinning.

'Old Leese represents a different kettle of fish. He's probably an old goat, and he *might* have thought that the Pratt was pennies from heaven. The only trouble about him is that he seems to have a hole-proof alibi for the time of the murder . . . he was having his elevenses with the Peels, the Parks, the Wells and old Togg, and all the parties confirm this separately . . . and, besides, even if he did do a satyr act with Miss Pratt, he's been a widower for twenty-seven years, and has been retired from his job for ten, so he isn't likely to fear blackmail. Besides, old pest though he may be, I don't see him hitting small, defence-less females with a brick. He reserves his big stuff for Miss Pew, as Jeffries explained, and even then it ain't lethal, it's only a lot of rude words.'

'Something of the truth will turn on Miss Nordle, I think,' Mrs. Bradley remarked. 'Your eliminations interest me very much. Do, pray, continue.'

'Miss Nordle? I really don't think we shall get much more out of *her*. She and Miss Pratt had had a very stiffish sort of toss-up—you know—high-hat stuff on the Pratt's part and unsuccessful rivalry on the Nordle's—but I simply cannot conceive of the Nordle bunging bricks. Changing the weed-killer for the vinegar, shoving the spoonful of arsenic in the coffee, even tying the string across the stairs—yes, I can imagine any of those, because they're in keeping with her sort of whining feminine psychology. But the wicketkeeper's busting of the stumps, or the technique of the smashing of cocoanuts—it's no good, I just can't conceive of it. It's completely out of character.'

'Yes,' Mrs. Bradley agreed. 'I know. The only trouble is, you see, that they *had* quarrelled, and it's the only real motive of a definite, credible, circumscribed kind that we've found.'

'Except, as I still contend, the general motive of any man on the coach, including Jeffries, in wishing to get rid of a nuisance.'

'You don't think that someone besides Miss Nordle may have felt envious of Miss Pratt's peculiar gifts?'

Gavin stared.

'Have we any evidence of that? That could be anybody! Anyhow, it all leaves us as we were, so I'm just going on with the sifting. The next move is to find out what those people were doing who haven't any visible alibi. Chief among these comes Miss Macklin. At least, that's my present view. Her story was particularly thin. But, as I say, I can't see this as a woman's crime at all. Oh, well, I'll ring up Mactavish to get busy over that shepherd she says she met. Let's go and get some dinner.'

But Miss Macklin proved to have a clean sheet. Mactavish broadcast for the shepherd. 'He clocked in at Crieff police station yesterday afternoon, and as soon as he was shown the snap of her with which old Uncle Togg had provided the police he swore to her at once, and he also came across with the time. He swore to the twite she said she'd seen,' said Gavin crossly, 'and added, apparently, that Robert Burns would have liked her. (This I, possibly in my ignorance, cannot imagine being likely!) He also referred to her as being 'sonsie', not an adjective I would ever have thought of employing, the Macklin being about as 'sonsie'—if I understand the vernacular aright—as a plump pork sausage. Still, every man to his taste, and Miss Macklin is definitely off the slate.'

'I am glad to hear it,' said Mrs. Bradley sincerely 'Music and murder are known to have gone hand in hand; but the simple bird watcher——'

'Our next job is to re-establish contact with Miss Baird and Miss Carter,' said Gavin. 'We got them to help us, I know, but it never actually transpired where they were or what they were doing at the time the murder was committed. This applies to several others, too.'

Miss Baird and Miss Carter shared a large, untidy house looking on to a gorse-quickened common. They had lived in it for twelve not completely unruffled but definitely quite contented years, and had bought the house with the intention of remaining there together.

They welcomed Gavin, thanked him for the message that had informed them of his intention to call, and hospitably strewed the belongings (with which most of the chairs were littered) on to a well-carpeted floor. They produced gin, bitters and sherry, and invited him to sit down and help himself.

'And now it's come,' said Miss Carter, forestalling all questions and adding a period to her announcement by taking a mouthful of gin. 'Dearie, the Bow Street runners have got us taped.' Gavin nodded solemnly and took out his notebook.

'Where were you from half-past ten until twelve on that Wednesday morning?' he asked. 'You know, the day of the murder.'

'I was with Mrs. Adderley,' said Miss Baird, evenly. Gavin was impressed and partly guessed what was coming.

'Miss Pew had been bullying her and upsetting her,' Miss Baird continued, 'and she came into the lounge where I was reading and began to tell me about it. But she also began to cry. That was rather awkward, so I took her up to my room, which, luckily, the maids had just finished with, and I gave her some brandy, and a spot of eau-de-Cologne behind the ears, and made her tell me her life story. It's the old one about the absolutely untrained middle-class woman whose husband died without providing for her. We talked until nearly twelve, and then I took her down to the lounge again, and ordered cocktails, and by lunch time she was just about ripe to give Miss Pew a piece of her mind. Why, in these days, anybody ever takes on the job of being a companion to a cross old maiden lady of that type I just can't think. I'd sooner wash doorsteps, myself, or do a job in a factory. Anyway, she cooled off again, because when we got down Miss Pew wasn't there.'

'Oh, yes. Where *was* Miss Pew?' asked Gavin. Although both he and Mactavish, guided partly by Mrs. Bradley, had decided that Miss Pew knew nothing whatever about the murder, including the time at which it had been committed, he had looked at that gap in his notebook which came opposite her name, and had speculated upon her probable occupation during the criminal hour. But for Mrs. Bradley's veto, he would have asked her about it long enough before this.

Miss Carter looked at Miss Baird, and then said with a reminiscent grin:

'Miss Pew? Oh, it was a put-up job between Catherine and myself. She was to comfort poor old Adderley . . . we were both most terribly sorry for the long-suffering old stupid . . . and I was to take on Miss Pew, and—and— well, give her something to think about besides bullying people and making herself a general pestilence.'

'Ah!' said Gavin, gazing at the point of his pen. 'And you took her . . . where?'

'Oh, for a ride of a sort,' said Miss Carter. 'I led her up

the garden, you know. She deserved it. Get her to tell you the details. I'd love to be there when she does. Oh, dear, she *was* cross. I expect she still is, come to that. I had fun.' Her blue eyes looked reminiscently into the purple past.

'Well, now for Miss Pew to confirm all that,' said Gavin. Miss Pew lived in a very handsome flat in what she was accustomed to refer to as the best part of Finchley.

'I suppose I can scarcely blame Miss Carter for the actual trouble I encountered,' she said, 'but I do blame her for her very thoughtless and ill-considered action in leading me into such a difficult, equivocal and embarrassing situation, and then of fleeing from it in that heartless, selfish way.'

'If you wouldn't mind just telling me what happened,' said Gavin, with all the tact at his command. 'You see, Miss Pew, the time was crucial, and although nobody would *dream* of suspecting a lady of *your* probity, Miss Carter's case is rather different. She seems, if I may say so, a Bohemian type, and such people are often unstable. I am sure you would not wish to see her get into any trouble when a word from you would be quite sufficient to clear her.'

Miss Pew thought it over. Her thin and wrinkled lips tightened. She distended her nostrils.

'Fighting fit,' thought Gavin. 'What the hell *did* they get up to? Not that I care, so long as it's something which clears them off my list.'

'She deserves to get into trouble; into very serious trouble,' said Miss Pew.

'But hardly with the police, I hope,' said Gavin, summoning what he believed to be an avuncular and playful smile. It was entirely wasted on Miss Pew, who underlined a thought she had had for some time in her mind, that Scotland Yard was not the entirely reliable institution she had always believed it to be.

'I am not at all certain about *that*,' she tartly rejoined. 'But I will tell you what she did, and then you may judge for yourself what action you ought to take. I certainly think she deserves a reprimand, but no doubt you are too young and inexperienced to make it sharp enough. It would be the business of your superiors, no doubt.'

'No doubt, Miss Pew,' replied Gavin, adding a rider to himself that he would shortly invite old Mr. Leese to take some refreshment at his expense. Jeffries' report of the old gentleman's descriptive epithets gave him pleasure to remember.

'Yes, well, to my evidence. She invited me to come for a ride in a private car,' continued Miss Pew. 'I naturally thought that one of the gentlemen was to drive, but, having accepted, I would not go back on my promise, even when, to my great surprise, I discovered that to begin with the car was not even hired . . . we had to walk into the town to an unsavoury little garage for that!'

'Dear me!' said Gavin. 'Too bad! But these writer people are very casual. Do, please, go on.'

'To be brief,' said Miss Pew, 'we set off, she at the wheel, I on the rear seat where I thought I should be more comfortable than in front. Besides, I am not accustomed to having anyone but my chauffeur and Mignonette Adderley at the front of my car. I invariably occupy the back seat. It looks so much more dignified.'

'Of course, of course,' said Gavin, easing his mind by

G

writing 'Silly old bitch' in shorthand in his official
notebook.

'We drove off,' continued Miss Pew, 'at a reasonable
enough pace (I must admit), and proceeded uphill through
very wild country until we came to a narrow road with
much moorland and mountain each side. The scenery was
good, although I have seen better, and I was beginning to
find mild pleasure in the drive when Miss Carter stopped
the car and suggested that we should get out for a short
time, as she thought the engine was boiling over, although
I myself could see no sign of this. Having no faith in hired
cars—particularly those hired by irresponsible young
women—I felt compelled to acquiesce, however, even
when Miss Carter suggested that we should walk for a
little. We crossed the road, took a very rough path and
gained the moorland. There was a boggy little stream, I
remember, and Miss Carter very wrongly and suddenly
left my side, as she had elected to leap across it in order to
explore some hillocks on the opposite bank.

'I was neither able nor willing to follow, so continued
on my own lines, and, soon having lost sight of Miss
Carter, I was picking my way without paying much heed
to direction (my faculties being engaged with trying to
make sure I did not stumble and fall down) when I heard
a sound not unlike the bellowing of a maddened bull.
Upon looking up, I found myself confronted by a most
hirsute man who (if I could have understood his *patois*)
seemed to be menacing me.

'Just then a covey of large birds rose almost from under
my feet. I was considerably startled. The truth was clear.
I was not only trespassing, but I was on a grouse moor,

where the young birds, no doubt, were in course of preparation for the September shooting.

'I expressed myself incoherently to the uncouth keeper (for such I suppose him to have been) and turned and walked back without giving him the satisfaction of believing that I was hurrying. Miss Carter was already in the car. She said she had sighted the keeper and had fled at once. *Not* the stuff of which heroines are made! We got back to the hotel at a quarter to one. I shall never speak to her again, and did not do so on the return journey. She had no right to place me in a position where I was obliged to *apologize* to an *underling*.'

'Thank you very much, Miss Pew,' said Gavin gravely. 'That has been extremely helpful. You will realize, I am sure, that you have now completely exonerated not only Miss Carter but yourself.'

'I should not have told such a revolting story otherwise,' said Miss Pew, sitting up very rigidly in her armchair. 'I am not altogether a fool, young man.'

Gavin almost began to respect her.

'Of course, we'll have to get confirmation at that garage and from the keeper,' he observed. 'But I haven't the slightest doubt that she's telling the truth.'

'I'm absolutely sure of it,' said Mrs. Bradley.

'That leaves us with Miss Bernard and Miss Cann. Miss Cann is much the likelier, from the point of view of strength and her training in throwing cricket balls, and from what we know of her temperament, but Miss Bernard strikes me as being the more noxious of the two. What say you?'

'Mrs. Cassock's mental condition is much improved,'

said Mrs. Bradley. Gavin looked at her questioningly. 'I was wondering whether you would be prepared to supply police protection for her.'

'Eh? Oh! Oh, I see. But you don't think the murderer would risk taking a slam at her, do you?'

'*I* would, if I were the murderer,' Mrs. Bradley briskly replied. 'Very soon it may be the murderer's life or Mrs. Cassock's, to my way of thinking, if the murderer gets the slightest inkling that Mrs. Cassock may soon be equal to telling the police what she saw.'

'What exactly goes on, then?' asked Gavin, impressed by Mrs. Bradley's arguments.

'At present, under light hypnosis, (which we could not get her to accept at first), we are bringing to the surface those incidents in Mrs. Cassock's past which have created the mental unbalance. Now this stage will work backwards, as it were, and, if good fortune is with us, Mrs. Cassock may be restored more or less to normality.'

'You say "restored more or less." You mean the cure won't be complete?'

'Who can say? Mrs. Cassock is a difficult subject. She is both secretive and unstable, and this seems to be her normal state. Such people are always inclined to be nervous and rather morose, and are liable to have a relapse. Our work is still in its infancy. It is always a truism that the more we know the more we realize what we *don't* know, but in the case of mental regeneration it is an absolute truth.'

'It isn't like you to be pessimistic.'

'That is not pessimism. It is a fact. A fact can be neither pessimistic nor optimistic in itself. It is its application which gives rise to emotion. I admit that I *am* worried. Mrs. Cassock is in grave danger, I would say, the moment she remembers the murder clearly, and that may be at any time now.'

'Well, let's cut the Gordian knot. As soon as you're sure she remembers seeing it done, let's confront her with the only two people we have left, and let her take her pick.'

'That might save her life, but it might permanently unseat her reason. She is a suicide type, remember. There would be no justification for saving her life from the murderer in order to let her take it herself.'

'Oh, Lord!'

'Yes,' said Mrs. Bradley sympathetically. 'In other words, we must lay the murderer by the heels before Mrs. Cassock recovers.'

'Of course, there's still Miss Nordle,' said Gavin. 'What was she doing after her putting-green game with Mrs. Amesby and Mrs. Hocking was over? *They* went off to have coffee, but what did *she* do?'

'I *think*,' said Mrs. Bradley, 'that she chased Bert into Dunblane.'

'Well, I'll knock Miss Bernard off first, and then we can see.'

Miss Bernard was run to earth at her kennels in Essex. She was, at the moment of Mrs. Bradley's arrival with Gavin, taking the temperature of a Lakeland terrier, and her friend, Miss Moxon, refused to disturb her during this delicate and slightly unseemly operation.

'He's a show dog,' Miss Moxon explained, 'and Bernie isn't quite satisfied about him. She's terribly conscientious, don't you know. His owner left him here a fortnight ago to be given a final polish up, but he began to scratch a bit this morning, so she thought she'd better take his pulse and his temperature. She'll be in in a minute. Will you have a shandy or something? I *think* there's some beer about somewhere. If you like I'll go and have a look.'

Her guests refused this lukewarm invitation, at which she seemed greatly relieved, and she soon left them and shortly returned with her friend.

'Sorry to keep you waiting, I'm sure,' said Miss Bernard, 'but I had to have a good wash. Patterdale Abbey Fell will have to be dosed,' she added to Miss Moxon. 'I suspect a worm. Isn't it a curse.'

'Oh, dear!' said Miss Moxon. 'He'll vomit if I dose him. He did before.'

'Not if you talk to him properly. He's a sensible dog, and hasn't been spoilt since we've had him. Now that new Chow is a brute. Besides, his coat's not good enough, and you know how that woman stampedes. You'll have to give him his powders. He likes you better than me.'

Gavin tactfully broke in upon this absorbing and professional conversation.

'I'm doing a round-up of the coach party in their own houses,' he said smoothly. 'Just a routine check, you know. Could you both cast your minds back to that Wednesday when you were all at Blaneden? You'd arrived on the Monday night, I think.'

The two concentrated. Miss Bernard's hair, Mrs. Bradley noticed, was badly in need of a wash. Her care for her charges, she reflected, seemed to take up most of her time.

RECAPITULATION BY THOSE CONCERNED

'Yes,' said Miss Moxon, 'I've got it! Bernie, you remember, don't you? The Inspector is talking about the day Miss Pratt was murdered.'

They exchanged glances. Then Miss Bernard got up.

'Just to avoid any suggestion of collusion between us,' she said, 'I think our answers had better be taken separately.'

Gavin smiled.

'You have saved my having to make the suggestion,' he said. 'Miss Moxon first, then, please.'

Miss Bernard went on, remarking over her shoulder, as she went, that she supposed she might as well begin clipping Pudel Ludwig Schloss, or he would never be ready in time.

'What do you want to know?' demanded Miss Moxon, as soon as the door was shut. Gavin took out his notebook and turned over the leaves.

'I'm re-checking alibis,' he said. 'Will you kindly tell me, all over again, exactly what you did on that Wednesday between breakfast and lunch?'

'Very well, then. I only hope I can remember it properly, or I suppose you'll put the handcuffs on me at once!' She laughed, but she sounded nervous. Gavin made no response of any kind. Miss Moxon waited to give him time to speak, but when he did not she went on: 'After breakfast I played tennis with Mr. and Mrs. Viccars and Miss Wells. We played until almost lunch time. And, by the way, in case you want to know, Bernie really *had* hurt her wrist that day, and that's why she wasn't my partner.'

Gavin respected loyalty. He nodded kindly. He went to the door, opened it and called out Miss Bernard's name.

'Just to make sure we don't tip each other the wink, I suppose,' said Miss Moxon cheerfully. Gavin stood in the doorway until Miss Bernard called back that she was just coming. She was as good as her word. She came in, handed the clippers she was carrying to Miss Moxon, sat down, and lit a cigarette.

'And now?' she said. 'Oh, have one of these, won't you? . . . Or don't you smoke? You don't? Oh, good!'

'What can you tell us about your movements on that Wednesday at Blaneden when you hurt your wrist?' asked Gavin.

'My movements?'

'Yes.'

'I knew this was coming. I've been waiting for it. It was quite too much to expect that you'd be able to leave us alone. Do you think I might have hurt my wrist killing Miss Pratt? Is that the idea?'

This straightforward query took Gavin aback. He did not immediately reply. Mrs. Bradley chuckled.

'Baldly and boldly put,' she observed, gazing with interest at the dog-woman.

'Well, it's best put that way, of course,' said Gavin. 'Come clean, Miss Bernard. I'll admit at once that I don't suspect you of the murder, but we're getting the thing whittled down, and you're almost the only person left on my list whose movements on the day in question are not accounted for.'

'The trouble is,' said Miss Bernard, 'that I've got no witnesses.'

'That would not necessarily cause me to disbelieve what you say.'

'Thanks a lot. Well, I hurt my wrist before breakfast trying to shove the bedroom window up at the bottom, so that when Moxie suggested tennis I had to cry off. It was all right because she got into a foursome instead. Cathleen Wells and the Viccars wanted another player, and asked her to fill in the gap. She's good, you know—at tennis, I mean. No, I mean she's altogether good.'

'We don't need your assurance,' said Gavin pleasantly. 'We have nothing against Miss Moxon.'

'Well, when Moxie had gone off to help them bag a court,' Miss Bernard continued, 'I went back to the bedroom and had another go at my wrist with hot and cold water. Then tied it up in a wet handkerchief. That's the idea, you know. I suppose I was quite ten minutes doing this, and the chambermaid came in while I was there and backed out again. But, of course, her statement won't help me unless Miss Pratt was killed at about ten o'clock or soon after, and I suppose she wasn't killed until at least eleven. She couldn't have been, could she?'

Gavin did not reply to this. He made a note, and then asked:

'How do you know it was about ten when the maid came in?'

'I heard it strike from the cathedral tower, and the maid came in soon after . . . about five minutes after, not more. At least, that is my recollection.'

'Please go on.'

'Well, I felt a bit at a loose end after that. I can't bear watching tennis. I don't even like playing it much, only Moxie is rather keen. It's all give and take when you're partners like we are, you see. Nothing works out right, otherwise, so when she wants tennis, I play.'

'Yes?'

'I doodled about in the bedroom, hoping the maid would come back. You see, then we could have had a gossip. People don't like me much. . . . I think my appearance puts them off and, anyway, I'm not sociable. I only like dogs and old Moxie . . . but I can always get on with maids. They're damned good judges of character, I consider. However, she didn't come back, so after the cathedral clock had chimed out the half-hour I went down to the lounge and peered about, but old Togg was in there, so naturally I didn't go in. I went down to have a look at the swimming bath, but nobody was using it and, anyway, I can't swim, so I left it by the garden door and went on up through the trees at the back of the hotel, through the garden.'

Gavin scribbled busily.

'Yes?' he said, on a slightly incredulous note.

'There was a fence at the top,' said Miss Bernard. 'I walked alongside it, first one way and then the other, until I came to a gate. It led on to a little path through a tiny field, and then there was a deep, dry ditch and I crossed it and got into a wood. From the wood I got on to the road, because if I hadn't done that there would have been another field to cross, and I was afraid I might be trespassing if I crossed it.'

'Just a minute, Miss Bernard,' said Gavin. Rapidly he turned back the pages of his notebook. He nodded, having found his place, and again looked at her keenly. 'Any possible chance of confirming all this?' he asked. 'You see,

I'm sure you went the walk, but another member of the party had done an almost identical stroll earlier in the day. What we've got to establish is whether you can prove that you took it *on that particular morning*. I'll be perfectly frank with you. If you *did go up* there on that Wednesday you would be a most unlikely suspect for the murder. Now, is there any way in which you can establish this alibi?'

Miss Bernard shook her head.

'I don't see how,' she said. 'The only thing that could confirm it can't speak, and it wouldn't know which day it was, anyhow.'

'A dog, I presume? Is that so?'

'Yes, it is. I went on up to the farm and made friends with a smooth-haired collie.'

'Did no one see you?'

'No, I'm afraid there was nobody. The dog was at the gate of the farmyard and nobody came that way at all, so far as I can tell you. There was a bearded collie by the cartshed, but that was chained up.'

'How long do you think you were up there?'

'With the dog? Oh, twenty minutes or more. I can always talk to a dog. After all, it's my job, you see.'

'Thank you, Miss Bernard,' said Gavin, standing up. 'I'm positive she's told us the truth,' he added to Mrs. Bradley, as they walked past the kennels to the road. 'But I wish someone had seen her on that walk. We can't cross her off on her own uncorroborated evidence.'

'There might be the smallest chance that somebody on the farm *did* see her,' said Mrs. Bradley. 'It is worth while to call up Inspector Mactavish, I think, and you should do so without losing time.'

'*You* think she's innocent, then?'

'Instinct tells me that she is, but instinct is not infallible.'

'No, of course not. I say, though, she's rather an odd type, wouldn't you say?'

'Unusual, but not *odd*.'

'Jeffries slipped up on her character. There can't be any doubt about that. He doesn't seem to have had a good word to say of her, according to those notes you showed me when you had made a précis of the information you got from his letters.'

'It is not to be expected that a man of Mr. Jeffries' age should be able to make an unbiassed judgment of a rather unattractive woman, especially of one who looks and smells as though a bath would improve her chances of social success,' said Mrs. Bradley.

Gavin laughed.

'At any rate, her lack of charm isn't going to persuade me into believing she murdered Miss Pratt,' he said decidedly. 'I'm absolutely positive she didn't.'

'I agree. I entirely agree. Besides, perhaps I ought to emphasize the fact that I've known now for quite a while who did.'

'As I've no intention of laying myself open to be snubbed, I shan't ask any questions,' said Gavin, grinning. 'My own instinctive bet, of course, is either a man or Miss Cann, but so far there's nothing to show it. Still, I don't want your conclusions until I can prove them.'

'Well, I'm glad Mrs. Cassock is under police protection,' said Mrs. Bradley, 'as I can't induce her to live at my clinic. And if you're going to bet on Miss Cann, we'll see her next. And then I want to challenge old Mrs. Binns with an entry from poor Miss Durdle's diary.'

'Miss Durdle and Mrs. Binns? Good heavens! You don't suspect either of *them!*'

'You spoke of discrepancies, child. I should be sorry to think that, in this case, *none* existed.'

A short time elapsed—a couple of days—and then Gavin called up Mrs. Bradley with the news of another tested and proved alibi.

'I say,' he said, 'you know Miss Bernard told us that she made friends with a smooth-haired collie up at that farm behind the hotel? It turned out, when Mactavish went up there to see whether anybody could swear to having seen her, that nobody had, but the Wednesday of Miss Pratt's death was the only day this particular dog was at the farm! All the farm collies are the bearded type, whatever that is! What do you think of that for sheer coincidence, though? Moreover, the dog didn't arrive until ten and he went home with his owner, a cousin of the farmer, at twelve. Talk about casting your bread upon the waters! Miss Bernard being a dog enthusiast, I mean, and remarking upon the smooth-haired collie. In other words, from being in the outer darkness of not having any alibi at all she turns out to have the most cast-iron one, almost, of the lot!

So now to see what happens to Miss Cann. If it's got to be a woman . . . and I presume you are sticking firmly to this utterly unpopular view . . . Cann would be my pick. She's got the strength and the training and, according to Miss Macklin, the willpower and bad temper for the kind

of slosh that killed Miss Pratt. I think, therefore, that we
have reached the end of the journey. I still don't ask
you for your conclusions, however. A hard-working
police officer has his pride. Besides, I *must* have a case for
a jury.'

By application to the Ling Association, Mrs. Bradley's
secretary, Laura Menzies, had begun a long process of
running Miss Cann to earth. She was not quite what she
had represented herself to be, for the Ministry had dis-
pensed with her services as a regional organizer of physical
education some six months before the beginning of the
Scottish tour. It was by devious means, therefore, that
Laura had managed to discover where she was and what
she was doing.

She was acting as relief physical training organizer to a
factory club in East London. It was a good job, as far as
salary was concerned, and was easy enough, since the girls
who came to the classes were volunteers only, and no
pressure was brought to bear upon those who did not
choose to attend.

'Why did you give us a wrong idea of the work you do?'
asked Gavin. Miss Cann shrugged her powerful shoulders.

'I'm a snob, I suppose,' she said. 'I know my work ought
to be important, and I suppose, in a way, it is, but when
you've always been in schools a factory doesn't seem very
strong beer.'

'Explain that, please.'

'I can't. It's the Old School Tie, I suppose. What do
you want me for, anyway?'

'I'm doing a routine check-up of everybody in the coach party, and I find that I have no account of your movements at the time of Miss Pratt's death.'

'What time was that?'

'What were you doing on that Wednesday morning between ten and one, Miss Cann?'

'I haven't the foggiest idea.'

'Come, now. You were at Blaneden. The day was Wednesday. You moved off to Aberdeen on the Thursday. Can you help me?'

'The Wednesday at Blaneden? Oh, just a minute! I kept a log of that Scottish tour.'

She went off, and shortly returned with a little book. She flicked over page after page.

'A diary? What an excellent idea,' said Mrs. Bradley. Miss Cann made no response until she found the place she wanted.

'Here you are, look,' she said. Gavin took the small book and studied the entry she showed him.

'You realize that anything you say can be proved or disproved very easily?' he said. Miss Cann tossed a horse-like head.

'You're welcome to try to disprove it,' she said with a snort. The entry read as follows:

'Wednesday, another Wednesday. Too far from either end of the week. One feels lost, stolen and strayed. Lost from grace, stolen from the pursuit of happiness, and strayed from the true fold. Ah, me! What will become of me in this wicked, ungrateful world? To begin with, I suppose I'll go along this morning and have a look at that camp.'

'That doesn't help very much,' said Gavin, handing the little book back.

'It helps to establish my innocence,' Miss Cann retorted. 'If my state of mind was such that I made that entry, I submit that I was not in the mood for murder.'

'You understand, then, what kind of a mood one needs for murder?' Mrs. Bradley immediately inquired. Miss Cann swallowed. Then she replied:

'Alas, yes!'

Gavin did not press her. Instead he said, speaking gently:

'Well, as your journal does not help us, Miss Cann, how about an account of your movements?'

Miss Cann gave a sudden, embarrassing but quite convincing giggle.

'You'll think me insane,' she said, 'but, at any rate, it's easily proved. I was so fed up—almost suicidal, in fact—that I had a busman's holiday.'

'Did some coaching or something, do you mean?'

'Not exactly. I'd found out where a company of Scouts were in camp. I went along there . . . you soon get browned off with sitting still in a coach and just glowering at scenery, don't you? . . . and so I went and umpired a baseball match, that's all. I got there at eleven and left at half-past twelve, when the boys were to have their lunch. I can give you the Scoutmaster's address, too, because he asked me whether I would join them in London at some time. They come from the East End, near Deptford. Nice kids! There you are. I think he'll swear to me all right. Here's my passport photograph to show him. Unlike many such, it's quite a reasonable likeness.'

'And that's that,' said Gavin, after they had left. 'Where do we go from here? Because I'm positive Mactavish will find that she's told us the truth.'

'To the murderer,' replied Mrs. Bradley. 'What would you say are the chief pointers to guilt?'

'Means, motive and opportunity, of course. Oh, and discrepancies in one's story, plus the manufacture of false evidence and the provision of immaterial clues.'

'Very well. Think it out, child.'

'I've tried to. I can't. You see, if it wasn't Miss Cann, and if all the others stand Sam for one another's alibis—except, of course, there's Miss Nordle. You think she went after Bert to Dunblane, but we haven't proved it yet.'

'We haven't asked Bert,' said Mrs. Bradley.

'Anyhow, so long as the two Miss Tooleys and old Mrs. Binns, as well as Miss Durdle, stand fast to their story that they were all in the cathedral at the crucial time, that's that. Of course, you know, apart from motive, there's the question of temperament, and that brings us back to Mrs. Cassock. And if it weren't for her alibi vouched for by old Miss Pew (and those two *can't* be in collusion) I think I'd bet on Miss Carter.'

'Miss Carter? You see her as a potential murderer?'

'I most certainly do. She's got the temperament all right, I should say, and she's got the boldness.'

'I know. But I thoroughly and completely agree with you that she and Miss Pew would never be in league to give one another an alibi, and to go on with I should always suppose a modern writer of detective stories to be the very last person on earth to commit a murder.'

'Why? I should think she'd have knowledge and wit enough to plan out something pretty foolproof.'

'To *plan* it out, yes, I agree. But she would never dare to carry out the plan. She would be so much accustomed to inventing the fictional murderer's mistakes that she would lack the necessary self-confidence. She would be certain to imagine all the slips she might make, and to decide that the game wasn't worth the anxiety it would cause her. Besides, her instincts——'

'Would have been sublimated. I know that one, and I don't believe it. I think a writer of murder stories could be just as murderous as anybody else. But I do think we ought to have another good look at Mrs. Cassock. I know we've fixed the time of the murder from her dramatic perform-ance on top of the cathedral tower, but I wonder whether there might not have been a catch in that.'

'I have always kept an open mind about it, child. She *could* have had time to knock Miss Pratt on the head and then stage her performance. Jeffries, who ran out after her that morning, lost track of her, you will re-member, from ten o'clock until he saw her on the tower, and the medical evidence, as always, gives ample leeway.'

'It was a pity she wasn't seen by the bus conductor. Mactavish found out that he was on the top deck collecting the fares, and she must have got off after about a couple of hundred yards, and could not have paid. In other words, there's only Jeffries' word for it that she got on a bus at all, apart from those two market women that Mactavish dug out, but who seemed to be rather vague in their descriptions. One thing—the driver of that car swears to Jeffries. Mactavish has worked pretty hard to contact these people. I'd like the case to clear itself up, if only for *his* sake.'

'There is little doubt of that now, child.'

'I wish we could trace that ciné-camera. You know, it's very odd, the way that disappeared. Mactavish has combed the place, including dragging the river, but there's never the slightest sign of it.'

'I wonder how soon your people will find that Scoutmaster and his boys,' Mrs. Bradley remarked. At that moment the telephone rang. Gavin picked it up.

'They've found them all right,' he grunted, 'and the description, taken separately from the Scoutmaster and three Patrol leaders, doesn't vary. Oh well, there can't be any doubt about *her*. More's the pity, I feel. She was rather a gem of a suspect.'

'Motive,' said Mrs. Bradley grimly. Gavin shook his head and then shrugged his shoulders.

'Yes, well, besides, I suppose she's just the kind to take a busman's holiday of that sort, when one comes to think of it,' he admitted. 'I wonder whether she'd have been quite so keen if the Scouts had been Guides, and their leader a stalwart young woman?'

'This cynicism does not become you,' said Mrs. Bradley, grinning. 'And I think you do Miss Cann an injustice. She lacks what is called the sporting spirit, but I should say that she is fanatically keen on games, and I don't think that she cares two hoots about men, as such.'

Gavin looked at her steadily.

'There's more in your last remark than meets the eye,' he said.

Mrs. Bradley cackled.

Mrs. Binns and Robert were both at home. Home, with them, meant a tall, narrow house, not unlike Mrs. Bradley's own place in Kensington. It overlooked Hyde Park, and gave added value to Gavin's Scottish impression that the Binns were people of substance.

'The ciné-camera?' said Robert. 'Oh, Mr. Peel has that, I'm almost sure.'

Gavin looked polite disbelief, although his own opinion coincided with this.

'There is nothing in our inquiry to suggest that,' he replied. Robert looked astounded.

'Of course there is,' he stated. 'And, of course, Commander Parks is phoney, isn't he? Ex-R.N. don't push silly notes under doors and give the game away.'

'That's *your* view,' Gavin observed. 'But which silly note are we talking about?'

'The one Miss Baird and Miss Carter got, of course. Miss Carter told me about it while we were chasing the caravan.'

'When?'

'Oh, one day at lunch. Mr. Jeffries never listened to what we said.'

'I see,' said Gavin slowly. 'Anything else you can tell us?'

'No,' said Robert regretfully. 'Not a thing.'

'You ought to be careful what you say,' said Gavin gravely. 'You might cause trouble, you know.'

'Yes, I want to,' said Robert. He looked at his grand-mother. She shook her head at him.

' "A boy's will is the wind's will, and the thoughts of youth are long, long thoughts," ' she observed. 'Why have you come here, Mr. Gavin?'

'To ask you one question,' said Mrs. Bradley.

'What is it?'

'Miss Durdle states in her diary that she saw you and the two Miss Tooleys in the cathedral on the morning of Miss Pratt's death.'

'Yes?'

'And you are quite certain that *you* did not see *her?*'

'I did not.'

'Did you see anybody else from the coach party?'

'No one else, apart from the two Misses Tooley.'

'Do you think any others could have been there and you not notice them?'

'No,' said old Mrs. Binns. 'I am perfectly certain that that would have been quite impossible. I had seen the cathedral before, and was much more interested in the visitors than in the architecture.'

'In that case, I think we will now go and see Miss Nordle,' said Mrs. Bradley.

Miss Nordle lived in lodgings. Her landlady opened the door and said that her lodger was in, and that it was the first floor front.

Gavin knocked at the bed-sitting-room door, and Miss Nordle opened it. She let out a little gasp when she saw who the visitors were.

'Routine stuff again, Miss Nordle,' said Gavin cheer-fully. 'May we come in? We're re-checking everybody's movements on the morning of Miss Pratt's death, and you're almost the last on our list.'

Miss Nordle, her normally silly manner replaced by the most obvious anxiety, held open the door and mechanically asked the visitors to sit down. Gavin, hitching up the knees of his trousers as he seated himself on the low settee bed—the room contained only two chairs and one of these was facing the window—glanced at Mrs. Bradley and nodded.

'Will you repeat the information you have already given us?' said the reptilian old woman in comforting tones. 'We have more information now than we had when we talked to you last time. We want to know whether you can substantiate some of our findings.'

Miss Nordle looked slightly dazed.

'Tell us all over again what you told us before,' said Gavin helpfully.

'I don't know as . . . I don't know that I can remember,' replied Miss Nordle miserably. 'Oh, if only I hadn't had those rows with poor Lilias she might have been alive to-day, and I'd be out of my dreadful troubles.'

'Think,' said Mrs. Bradley, persuasively. 'Breakfast, after breakfast, lunch. Take the affair in that order. First, try to remember getting up. Miss Pratt didn't share your room, did she? I think I understood that you had singles.'

'Yes, that's right,' agreed Miss Nordle. 'I had breakfast and then I . . . oh, and Lilias wasn't down to breakfast. Yes, I remember now. I didn't know what to do with myself, what with the stomach ache and everything, so I went out on to the putting green, thinking the fresh air and gentle exercise would do me good, and I knew we'd only move slowly, Mrs. Amesby and Mrs. Hocking being so . . . well, outsize in undies, as you might say, not wishing to sound coarse.' She giggled in almost her old manner and looked invitingly at Gavin. 'Because coarseness I have no use for, especially in front of gentlemen. Well, them being like what they are, I knew I wouldn't need to go in for exertion, my second day being quite as bad as my first, and that's where I did think Lilias rather unkind, her knowing I suffer like I do . . .'

'You played on the putting green with Mrs. Amesby and Mrs. Hocking, yes,' said Gavin, feeling that Miss Nordle's sufferings were rather beside the point. 'That's exactly what you told us before. Thank you, Miss Nordle. That's very helpful indeed. There's just one other small matter.' He smiled amiably at his victim. Miss Nordle suddenly looked smaller. In her eyes was extreme terror.

'Another small matter?' She seemed to choke on the words. The knobbly knuckles which Jeffries disliked so much were white with the tension of her clasped hands. Gavin could see that her thighs were shaking. He thought she might be going to faint.

'Yes. We have evidence, well-supported evidence, too, that Mrs. Amesby and Mrs. Hocking went off into the town when the game was over, and had coffee in a little restaurant. What did *you* do? . . . We know you didn't go with them.'

'I . . . oh, I . . . I remember. I thought them very rude and unkind. I did think they might have asked me to go with them as we'd all been playing together, but they sneaked off under pretence of wanting the toilet, and they didn't come back. So, well, I've got my pride. I don't ever

push myself in when not wanted. I waited a bit and then I
guessed they'd gone for morning coffee and pastries . . . no
wonder they've got those dreadful figures . . . so I went
straight to the cathedral and Miss Durdle will swear to me
being there.'

She drew an enormous breath.

'The cathedral. Oh, yes,' said Gavin pleasantly. 'All
right, Miss Nordle. That settles that. Now, when you left
the cathedral, where did you go?'

Miss Nordle, now obviously relaxed, had resumed her
normal expression and seemed to have regained her usual
size.

'Oh, in to lunch, of course,' she said. 'I was feeling
quite peckish by that time.'

'And who, besides Miss Durdle, was in the cathedral
with you? Anybody else from the coach? Whom else did
you see?'

'Oh, Mrs. Binns and, of course the two Miss Tooleys—
yes, they were there.'

'That corresponds with our records. Now, Miss Nordle,
to the point. You may have seen *them*, but, unfortunately,
neither Mrs. Binns nor the Miss Tooleys can actually
swear to having seen *you*. Can you explain that, please?'
He had taken out his notebook and now tapped on it with
his fountain pen.

'No, I can't! We were all there. That I'm certain of.
But, anyhow, Miss Durdle . . .'

'Of course. You and Miss Durdle, you think, can give one
another an alibi. Very well, we will see Miss Durdle, and
I think it would clear matters up if we took you with us.'

Miss Nordle looked apprehensive.

'But I don't know her all that well,' she began to protest. 'I mean, not to visit at her house.'

'Oh, that's all right,' said Gavin, easily. 'It isn't exactly a social call, you know.' He glanced at Mrs. Bradley, who had primed him. She nodded.

Miss Durdle received them in her usual manner.

'This is indeed an honour,'' she said, 'for you all to seek me out in my wee domain. I must record this visit in my diary.'

'Do,' said Gavin, cheerfully. 'Now, Miss Durdle, to brass tacks. We've brought Miss Nordle with us so that you can (if you think you ought to) substantiate her alibi. I ought to warn you,' he added, 'that what you say will be taken down and may be used in evidence.'

'Oh dear, that sounds very policemanish,' said Miss Durdle. 'I must commit it to my diary without delay. Do excuse me a moment while I go and get it. Used in evidence, I think you said. Quite a little adventure, isn't it?'

She was bustling off, but Gavin intercepted her.

'Just a minute, Miss Durdle. Possibly the diary will wait. Miss Nordle's alibi, first, please. I believe you made a mention of it in your diary.'

Miss Durdle sat down. Gavin sat between her and the door, Mrs. Bradley between her and the window, and Miss Nordle on an upholstered stool beside the empty fireplace.

'Miss Nordle was with me in the cathedral,' said Miss Durdle. 'And Mrs. Binns and the two Miss Tooleys were there. Yes, I remember it quite well. There had been a dreadful fuss about Mrs. Cassock on the tower.'

'And a murder had just been committed in the hotel garden,' said Mrs. Bradley. Miss Durdle looked at her vaguely.

'Oh, poor Miss Pratt, yes,' she said. 'But one can't help thinking she brought it upon herself, can one? So *very* free with the gentlemen! I *never* think it does for a girl to make herself cheap.'

Gavin gravely agreed.

'Now, Miss Nordle,' he said, 'do you still support Miss Durdle's statement that you and she were in the cathedral together?'

'Yes, oh, yes, of course I do!' cried Miss Nordle.

'Ah, then, we were being misled when one of the witnesses hinted to us that you went to Dunblane when your putting green game was over?'

Miss Nordle half got up, sat down heavily again, gulped twice as though she were going to choke, and broke out into noisy sobbing.

'I didn't do it! I didn't kill Lilias!' she cried.

'All right,' said Gavin. 'Thank you. Come along.'

Miss Durdle showed them out, her heavy, rather unintelligent visage creased in a perplexed and nervous smile.

'Can I go home now?' asked Miss Nordle, tearfully. Gavin shook his head.

'We have to visit the two Miss Tooleys,' he said. 'We mustn't leave anything to chance if we're going to prove your innocence.'

The drive to the Tooleys' flat was a short one, but there

was no doubt of Miss Nordle's terror at being confronted with the two sisters.

'I'm awfully sorry,' said Miss Sheila Tooley, looking away from Miss Nordle's white and tear-stained face, 'but I couldn't definitely say that I saw her and Miss Durdle in the cathedral that Wednesday morning.'

Her eyes met those of her sister, and both women looked even more uncomfortable than before.

'I think I *would* have said so, if it hadn't been for old Mrs. Binns,' said Miss Janet Tooley at last in a troubled voice. 'But she rang through about five minutes ago and told us to be careful.'

'Of course, there were quite a number of visitors there,' said Miss Sheila Tooley, after a half glance at her sister's tense expression.

'Don't let your good nature get the better of your memory,' said Mrs. Bradley drily.

'We never said we *did* see her, you know,' Miss Sheila Tooley added. 'We only swore to old Mrs. Binns, but when they came to us . . .'

'*They?*'

'Miss Durdle came too,' said Miss Janet Tooley unwillingly. 'She was such a poor old thing, and pitched us such a tale. . . . But I don't think I ever thought the police would question us about either of them.'

'Neither did I,' said her sister.

'Ah, then Miss Durdle is the one,' said Gavin. Mrs Bradley gazed admiringly at him. 'You knew it all the time,' he added accusingly. Miss Durdle herself supplied the answer to this question.

'I heard Miss Pratt telling everybody she was going to

meet Mr. Jeffries at the bottom of the garden,' she said. 'But he was mine, not hers, and so I told her.'

'Well,' said Gavin later, 'it was a bit odd, and rather interesting, that Jeffries' earliest reaction to Miss Durdle was to feel rather scared of her. Do you remember that she was the one who always seemed to be saying "Liar" instead of "Thank you," when he gave the coach-load any information? Of course, her plea of poverty was a complete myth. It's perfectly obvious that she always afforded the things she really wanted. I wonder what sort of nuisance Jeffries was when he insisted on taking her on that expedition she said she couldn't pay for? It must have interfered with her plans, because quite definitely she hadn't intended to go. My bet is that she had a deep scheme to kill Miss Pratt then instead of on the Wednesday, and it's possible that, if she had, we might never have caught her.

'Mind you, in one sense, the Pratt did ask for what she got. The Parks' row at Aberdeen was over his slight and probably harmless tendency to go wenching. Apparently Jeffries never spotted it; but, then, neither did he spot the discrepancy between Miss Durdle's avowed terror of lonely walks and that early morning one she took when he met her. I suppose she'd followed him.'

'Bless Mr. Jeffries' innocent heart!' said Mrs. Bradley. 'We must never allow him to know that he is *un homme fatal*.'

'A what?' asked Gavin, horrified. Mrs. Bradley cackled.

'He often gave the impression in his letters that he would like to murder Miss Pratt,' she said, 'and, of course, by proxy, he did. That merry jest, by which Bert, the driver, got Miss Pratt to the bottom of the hotel garden, was a red rag to a bull to poor Miss Durdle. She (as her diary plainly indicates) had appropriated Jeffries for herself. She even admits that now. And, of course, she wrote the note that was found. You remember? . . . The devil gives the elbow to such as this . . . or words to that effect?'

'But a woman of that age! And, all her life, until this awful business, so respectable! I can't quite swallow it, even now, you know.'

'Respectability stands very little chance of holding the balance against the curious fancies of emotionally-starved and middle-aged spinsters, child. The cruel Mr. Gilbert knew that. I have never really liked his librettos. And, in real life, look at the case of Miss Camille Holland of the Moat House Farm.'

'And there was no connection at all between the smuggling and Miss Pratt's death? Jeffries seemed to think there must be, and that the ciné-camera might have supplied the motive.'

'There seemed a strong probability at first that there was some connection,' Mrs. Bradley admitted. 'But one soon realized that the camera could have been (as indeed it was) appropriated without the necessity of committing murder. Robert was right. Mr. Peel had it. He has now confessed as much. He overheard Miss Pratt (no very difficult matter, apparently) boasting of her tryst with the incorruptible Dan, and he made his plans accordingly. It was easy enough to slip into Miss Pratt's room after he had watched her leave the hotel, take the camera, and extract the roll of film.

'No doubt he intended to replace it, but found no opportunity before the boat party set out for Leith. Then, when the fuss began over Miss Pratt's disappearance, the safest thing, it seemed to him, was to get rid of the camera. This he did by dropping it into the River Ness. Inspector Mactavish will, no doubt, recover it. By the way, Commander Parks appears to have been a stool-pigeon to the smugglers, but there is no doubt that he allowed them to cut him in for a small share of the gains. He knew that there was something illegal going on, although he won't really admit this. Incidentally, his title is merely an assumed one. He was never in the Navy. Robert, who all the way through has shown himself to be an acute psychologist, was right about that, as about several other things.'

'And had Miss Pratt taken a picture that might have been damaging to the smugglers?'

'No. She had taken one which showed Mr. Parks and Mr. Peel at tea with two unknown and rather overdressed ladies when they were supposed to be inspecting the boat. Mr. Peel seems to have told Bert that it would have been more than his life was worth to let his wife see it. He tried to bribe Bert to steal it from Miss Pratt's room, but Bert, not unnaturally, declined to go within a mile of so equivocal a destination.'

Gavin laughed, but his laughter suddenly chilled on him, and he asked:

'Was it Miss Durdle who wrapped up the body in those rugs and carried it to the motor-coach?'

'Oh yes. It was quite in character, really, although it seems a desperately dangerous thing to have done. She says she didn't think it was nice to leave Miss Pratt there all alone when all the others were going over the Devil's Elbow Pass.'

'Good heavens! She must be mad!'

'Poor Miss Durdle! There's a devil in a box in all of us, my dear Gavin. The lucky ones are those who can sit on the lid.'

VINTAGE

MORE VINTAGE MURDER MYSTERIES

EDMUND CRISPIN

Buried for Pleasure
The Case of the Gilded Fly
Holy Disorders
Love Lies Bleeding
The Moving Toyshop
Swan Song

A. A. MILNE

The Red House Mystery

GLADYS MITCHELL

Speedy Death
The Mystery of a Butcher's Shop
The Longer Bodies
The Saltmarsh Murders
Death and the Opera
The Devil at Saxon Wall
Dead Men's Morris
Come Away, Death
St Peter's Finger
Brazen Tongue
Hangman's Curfew
When Last I Died
Laurels Are Poison
Here Comes a Chopper
Death and the Maiden
Tom Brown's Body
Groaning Spinney
The Devil's Elbow
The Echoing Strangers
Watson's Choice
The Twenty-Third Man
Spotted Hemlock
My Bones Will Keep
Three Quick and Five Dead
Dance to Your Daddy
A Hearse on May-Day
Late, Late in the Evening
Fault in the Structure
Nest of Vipers

MARGERY ALLINGHAM

Mystery Mile
Police at the Funeral
Sweet Danger
Flowers for the Judge
The Case of the Late Pig
The Fashion in Shrouds
Traitor's Purse
Coroner's Pidgin
More Work for the Undertaker
The Tiger in the Smoke
The Beckoning Lady
Hide My Eyes
The China Governess
The Mind Readers
Cargo of Eagles

E. F. BENSON

The Blotting Book
The Luck of the Vails

NICHOLAS BLAKE

A Question of Proof
Thou Shell of Death
There's Trouble Brewing
The Beast Must Die
The Smiler With the Knife
Malice in Wonderland
The Case of the Abominable Snowman
Minute for Murder
Head of a Traveller
The Dreadful Hollow
The Whisper in the Gloom
End of Chapter
The Widow's Cruise
The Worm of Death
The Sad Variety
The Morning After Death